# GHOSTS OF WAR

## Restless Spirits of Soldiers, Spies, and Saboteurs

# GHOSTS OF WAR

## Restless Spirits of Soldiers, Spies, and Saboteurs

### JEFF BELANGER

ROSEN
PUBLISHING

New York

This edition published in 2009 by:

The Rosen Publishing Group, Inc.
29 East 21st Street
New York, NY 10010

Cover design by Nelson Sá.

## Library of Congress Cataloging-in-Publication Data

Belanger, Jeff.
Ghosts of war : restless spirits of soldiers, spies, and saboteurs / Jeff Belanger.
      p. cm.—(Haunted: ghosts and the paranormal)
Includes bibliographical references and index.
ISBN: 978-1-4358-5177-1 (library binding)
1. Ghosts. 2. War—Miscellanea. I. Title.
BF1471.B45 2009
133.109—dc22

2008035432

*Manufactured in the United States of America*

First published as Ghosts of War: Restless Spirits of Soldiers, Spies, and Saboteurs by New Page Books / Career Press, copyright © 2006 by Jeff Belanger

# DEDICATION

Dedicated in loving memory of my grandfathers:

Machinist Mate, First Class, Edward W. Belanger Sr.,
United States Navy, who served in the South Pacific aboard
the USS *Currituck* a.k.a. the "Wild Goose" during World War II.

Sergeant First Class, Joseph Henry Chamberland,
United States Army, 1st Infantry Division,
who served in Northern France, Rhineland Ardennes,
Central Europe, and fought in the
Battle of the Bulge during World War II.

# ACKNOWLEDGMENTS

Discussing haunted battlefields, ships, airplanes, boats, and other war-related locations hits many nerves, and talking about ghosts in any context often makes people uncomfortable. But when these two subjects are put together, some people want nothing to do with them, which is a tragedy because there are stories to be told about real people, and there is history to be remembered. I'd like to thank those brave souls who were willing to discuss the battles, the people who fought and died, and the ghosts who play a role in keeping people coming back to these hallowed locations. In researching this book, many people trusted me with two subjects they hold sacred: history and the spiritual. I've worked very hard not to let them down.

Thank you to the folks at New Page Books who have been so supportive of me and my work. It's been a pleasure working with them, especially Michael Pye, Laurie Kelly-Pye, Linda Rienecker, and Ron Fry. Thank you also to my editor, Gina Talucci.

To my wife, Megan, who has not only learned that we simply must visit some haunted locations during every trip we take, but who has actually learned to enjoy and appreciate these sites. Thank you from the bottom of my heart. I couldn't do this without your support and help.

I also appreciate the many friends and colleagues who have given me so much help with this book. Thanks to Richard Senate, John Kachuba, Cody Polston, Stuart Edmunds, Richard Kimmel, and Lee Prosser. And of course, thank you to the many Ghostvillagers of the world who have passed through my Web site, *www.ghostvillage.com*, over the years. It's been wonderful to sit around the virtual campfire with you all learning from each other.

# CONTENTS

# FOREWORD

You don't have to believe in ghosts to enjoy Jeff Belanger's *Ghosts of War*. It seems ghosts are not attracted to places with dull histories, and ghost stories are certainly not told about humdrum people. In this volume, Belanger relates 29 tales of wartime violence and the ghosts these incidents have reportedly left behind. The battles, sieges, and assassinations are described in colorful prose that is obviously rooted in deep scholarship. They cover a period ranging from the 12th century wars of the Taira and the Minimoto clans in medieval Japan to the Bosnian War of 1992–95. The American Civil War turns out to be particularly rich in ghost-generating battles, with seven such incidents. World War II, Belanger writes, has resulted in six haunted places, including three ships. The tales of the battles alone make *Ghosts of War* a most worthwhile addition to any military history buff's library, but the ghosts add extra spice. The scariest of the ghost stories concerns Hoichi the Earless, a blind musician who wanted to learn about the last battle of the Taira. The most energetic of the ghosts is our own Mad Anthony Wayne, the Revolutionary War general who captured the British-held fort on Stony Point by leading 1,000 men with unloaded muskets on a night assault. Every New Year's Day, the legend has it, Mad Anthony leaves his grave in the suburban Philadelphia town of Radnor and rides 400 miles to Erie, then rides back before sunup. Why this wild ride? He's looking for his bones. And what happened to his bones? You'll have to read *Ghosts of War*.

—William Weir
Author of *50 Battles That Changed the World* and
*50 Military Leaders Who Changed the World*

# INTRODUCTION

You can't study ghosts and spirits without also exploring history. And you can't stand in the middle of a battlefield where thousands of people lost their lives in a very short period of time during a confrontation that may have changed the course of world events and not feel something. I'm not necessarily talking about a psychic impression or some New Age connection to the other side (though that's also possible)—I mean an understanding of what it must have been like for your fellow human beings (and maybe even your own ancestors) to give up their lives for the sake of gaining 50 feet of front line.

We need to stand at these hallowed locations and remember that the soldier who gave his life didn't do so because he felt 50 feet of line movement was worth dying for—he braved oncoming arrows, swords, bullets, mortar fire, and tanks because he believed his side was right. His homeland's way of life was at stake, and his family, friends, country-men, and comrades were depending on him.

Wars and battles are full of statistics, such as 51,000 dead and wound-ed at Gettysburg, and 3,000 dead at Edgehill Battlefield. Even more staggering, 60 million people died as a result of World War II when you include soldiers and civilians from every nation involved. But these are all just numbers, and numbers are cold. When you stand at the Vietnam

Veterans Memorial in Washington, D.C., you learn that the number of Americans killed in that conflict was 58,196. When you walk along the wall, you can see and touch the individual names. Each name represents a vast network of moms, dads, siblings, children, spouses, and friends who were crushed by the loss of this person.

*The Vietnam Memorial in Washington, D.C.*
*Photo by Jeff Belanger*

When soldiers die tragically for a cause they feel is bigger than themselves, an impression is made, and not just on the living people who knew them and have to go on without them; an imprint is left on the land, the boat, the spot where they perished.

Ghost sightings are common at the site of military conflicts because we can't forget what happened there. If you'll permit me a cliché: Those who don't remember history are doomed to repeat it. Phantom regiments of soldiers locked in battle, lone sentries still walking their patrols, and disembodied pleas for help are just some of the phenomena witnesses have reported in *Ghosts of War*.

While researching this book, I did encounter a few people who felt it was a dishonorable thing to suggest that a battleship or battlefield may be haunted by soldiers who fought and died there. Nothing could be further from the truth. Through ghostly encounters, we're going to remember those who fought, and we'll put names and sometimes faces to the spirits of these brave souls. We'll remove the ghosts from the cold file of "Killed in Action" statistics and get to know some of the people who helped shape battles, wars, and the world we live in today.

In researching certain battles of the United States Civil War for this book, I had the opportunity to speak with several reenactors—people who dress up in reproductions of Confederate and Union uniforms, complete with rifles, canteens, and tents from the bygone Civil War era. The reenactors often visit battle sites on the anniversaries of the conflict. They'll camp out for the weekend and live exactly the way the soldiers did back in the 1860s. If the fighting started at 10 AM, they'll be on the fields at 10 AM with muskets at the ready, replaying as closely as they can the actual events that took place there.

Many times Civil War reenactors experience ghosts. The witnesses I spoke with don't consider themselves psychic in any way—they just know what they saw, heard, and felt. By placing themselves in the uniform and at the location, and by understanding the details of the battle and the frame of mind of these long-dead soldiers, either consciously or subconsciously a Civil War reenactor is opening up to every impression left on the field.

I spoke to author and lecturer Richard Senate about this theory, and he had another additional thought: "I think that the whole experience of the reenactment tends to restimulate psychic energy or the leftover psychic traces. The reenactments themselves might act as a trigger." Maybe both the restimulation and frame-of-mind factors are working together to produce a higher rate of ghost sightings. No matter the cause, the effect is that war reenactors may be the most likely group of candidates to experience the supernatural on a consistent basis.

Some of the more progressive battle museums and preservation sites have come to not only accept their ghosts, but incorporate them into the program. Young schoolchildren may show up for an educational field trip expecting to be bored with history and statistics, but they suddenly perk up when they hear that a ghost may be about. The docents and tour guides quickly learn that their ghosts offer an innovative way to teach history. In learning history, we remember and understand the past. I can think of no better way than to honor and appease any restless spirits of battle.

Wars don't just leave ghostly impressions on the land and battle sites—they also affect a society's entire view on the supernatural. On Friday, March 31, 1848, in the small town of Hydesville, New York, the Spiritualist movement was born when Kate and Margaretta Fox heard an unexplained knock on their walls. The Fox sisters sensed some intelligence to these knocks and began communicating. From these knocks, the Fox sisters rose to fame and a new religion called Spiritualism, with spirit communication as its base, was started. After the United States Civil War ended in 1865, the Spiritualist movement saw an explosion in growth because so many families had lost loved ones during the war and people were desperate to try and reach out to their fallen kin. After the first World War, mediums and psychics were, again, sought to reach out to the spirits of dead soldiers. In the 1940s, after World War II, interest spiked once more. In today's uncertain geopolitical climate, with terrorism and wars on the minds of many, we're seeing this resurgence again.

Wars, the often senseless loss of life, and the rebuilding of lives and countries get people thinking about spirituality and their own mortality. Are people more prone to ghost encounters during periods of war and catastrophe? Maybe. There is certainly empirical evidence to suggest this. That's not to say ghosts don't appear during peacetime, but there is a noticeable increase during and after wars.

*Ghosts of War* is a closer look at history than I have done in the past. Because many times the ghosts who haunt battlegrounds are recognizable historical figures, it's important to set the stage with a look back at why each particular battle came to be and what the outcome meant. Inside these pages, we're going to meet the soldiers who served through their journal entries and memoirs, and we'll speak with historians, ghost hunters, and eyewitnesses to modern-day spirits at these hallowed locations.

There are people exploring haunted battle sites and even the very items of war such as medals, uniforms, and even machine parts from every conceivable angle. We have an undeniable connection to the past through this field of study. We pursue and explore both the history and the supernatural connection because battles have brought out the worst and the best in people, and there is much we can still learn even though the last shots may have been fired long ago.

For the sake of progress, some battlefields are in danger of being replaced by condominiums, strip malls, and parking lots. If these landmarks disappear, the wars that were fought there will drift further back into distant memory until one day, only the spirits will be left to testify as to what happened. It's important we pay attention to history and to the ghosts. Both have quite a bit to teach us about ourselves.

# *Part I*

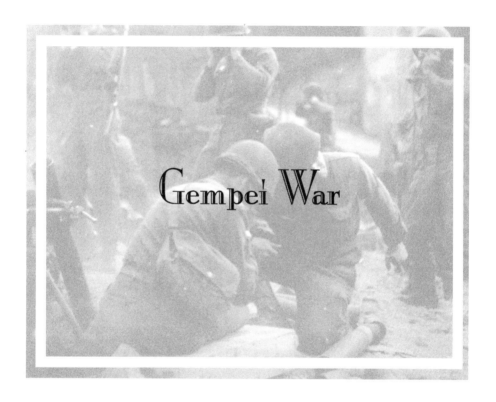

Gempei War

(1180–1185)

# 1

# DAN-NO-URA

**War:** Gempei War (1180–1185)
**Date of battle:** April 24, 1185
**Location:** Straits of Shimonoseki off the northern part of
Honshu, Japan, near the Inland Sea
**Participants:** The Taira (Heike) clan and their 500 boats against the
Minamoto (Genji) clan and their 850 boats

*In the sound of the bell of the Gion temple echoes the imper-
manence of all things . . . The proud ones do not last long, but
vanish like a spring night's dream. And the mighty ones, too,
will perish like dust before the wind . . .*
—*The Tale of the Heike*, circa 1371

The tale of the Taira clan has been told for centuries in Japan. The
Gempei War, and its final battle in the straits of Shimonoseki off the coast
of Dan-no-Ura, has been immortalized in verse in *The Tale of the Heike*,
which was spread orally by the biwa hoshi, or "lute priests." These lute-
playing bards told the tale for many years before it was finally dictated in
1371 by the Japanese bard Kakuichi. From there, the story became
standardized and the epic spread. Near the coastline in Dan-no-Ura is
a cemetery believed to be haunted by the last emperor from the Taira

clan, his family, and many of the samurai warriors who died trying to protect him on April 24, 1185. The story behind the ghosts is even more saddening than the spirits who may still wander the area.

The Gempei War was born during the Taira's rise to power. In 1180, the warrior Taira Kiyomori, whose actions helped his clan conquer their enemies, was sent to eliminate a thorn in the side of the royal court. The thorn was Minamoto Yoshitomo, a warrior from the powerful Minamoto clan. Taira Kiyomori brought the battle to Minamoto Yoshitomo on the sea—where the Minamoto clan was not used to fighting—and Taira Kiyomori proved to be the victor. Kiyomori spared the lives of Yoshitomo's three young sons—boys who would grow up to be powerful warriors and leaders in the Minamoto clan and who would harbor a powerful grudge against the clan who killed their father. After the battle, the Emperor rewarded Kiyomori with land in western Japan. The Taira clan ran a highly profitable trade with China and quickly grew wealthy and powerful, but the jealousy and hatred from the Minamoto grew stronger each year. When the call to the Gempei War was sounded in May 1180, the Minamoto quickly answered.

Wars are fought for many reasons but land, wealth, and power (often the three are synonymous) are always near the top of the list. The Taira were the ruling clan and had the power; the Minamoto were no longer content with their little corner of the empire. The Taira were slow to respond to the Minamoto uprising because they didn't take the grumbling and minor skirmishes as anything more than the occasional venting of frustration. The Taira felt the people in the empire were content for the most part and didn't want a war. But as the violence escalated, this opinion changed.

A year after the fighting had begun, the Minamoto presented an offer to Taira: split the land in half and have each family clan control their own part. But this offer was waved off, angering the Minamoto further. Between 1182 and 1183, a truce was forced as a poor harvest brought disease and starvation to the land; but battles picked up again in 1183. In the coming years, the Minamoto chipped away at the armies and land of the Taira, forcing them to retreat and regroup. Thousands were dying on the front lines of both sides. Minamoto pushed Taira to the sea, and in 1185 the final battle lines were being drawn.

The Taira set sail for Shido harbor with 500 boats. In one vessel was Antoku, the Taira child emperor, his grandmother, and guards. Both sides sensed a final battle was nigh. If the Taira lost, they would be decimated, and if they won, they would only live to fight another day. When the sun rose on April 24, 1185, the Minamoto set sail with 850 boats on the hunt for the Taira fleet. The two met at Dan-no-Ura. The battle began with a volley of arrows and both sides fought with determination. The Taira, though outnumbered, had the tide in their favor and were seeing success in battle—enemy ships were being sunk, and their samurai were fighting valiantly. But their hopes were soon dashed when one of their own switched sides during the battle. A Taira warrior named Taguchi Shigeyoshi made his way to one of the Minamoto boats and pointed out which Taira vessel held the child emperor. Nature also turned on the Taira as the tide switched in favor of the Minamoto boats that now took aim at the emperor's vessel. The Taira samurai saw the overwhelming force headed their way and chose to drown before allowing themselves to be taken prisoner. Armored men jumped into the chilly waters and allowed the weight of their protective gear to carry them to the bottom. Others threw the ship's anchors overboard and held onto the weight to speed their own trip to the ocean floor.

The emperor's grandmother scooped up Antoku, who didn't understand what was happening. She held him close to her chest as she carried him to the rail of the ship and told the child that a happier empire waited below the water. She jumped to both of their dooms. The Taira were completely defeated and the dawn of a new era of military leadership had begun.

With such a massive loss of life and a complete change of the region's leadership, it is no surprise the area of Dan-no-Ura is both revered and haunted. There is a great challenge in separating real ghostly legends and folklore from the influence popular fiction has had on this area and tale. *The Tale of the Heike* has influenced many novels, films, theatrical works, and art. So many modern bards have put their own spin on this story that the real facts and the fiction based on the legends have become intertwined. But both deserve some degree of attention.

One popular legend is that of Hoichi the Earless—a blind biwa hoshi (lute-playing priest) who came to the Akama-jingu Temple, which is dedicated to Emperor Antoku, to learn *The Tale of the Heike*. To learn the tale, Hoichi knew he needed to know about the Taira, and there could be no better places to learn than the area where the battle was fought and at the temple dedicated to the child emperor. Hoichi's skills at playing and singing the epic tale grew. One night around midnight, Hoichi heard the approach of what he could only assume was a samurai, (considering the clink-clank of armor and the gruff way in which the warrior called out Hoichi's name). The samurai told Hoichi that his lord had requested Hoichi to perform for him that night. The blind minstrel was happy to oblige and was led into town and to the shore. Hoichi heard the ocean waters and couldn't understand why a nobleman would be staying near the coast. But soon he heard large doors open and he was led into a room full of people. The lute priest heard the swish of silk gowns and the mumbles of aristocracy.

Hoichi sat down and played the performance of his life. His audience was moved to tears upon hearing the climax of the battle when so many samurai and the young emperor himself dove to their deaths in a last stand for honor. At the conclusion of his song, Hoichi was told he would come back the next two evenings, but that he should speak of this to no one. After the third performance, he was promised a great reward. The samurai then returned the minstrel to the temple.

What Hoichi didn't realize was that the priest who oversaw the temple came back later that evening and discovered Hoichi was missing. The next morning when he found Hoichi sleeping he woke him up and asked him where he had been—the old priest was worried about his young friend. Hoichi told the priest he simply went out and couldn't say anything more.

That day the priest in charge of the temple asked one of his monks to sit outside and watch for Hoichi to leave. When midnight came, this servant watched Hoichi pick up his biwa, appear to take the arm of some unseen person, and walk out of the temple gate. The servant ran after Hoichi but couldn't find him. The servant ran through town searching the alleys and streets, but found no trace. As the servant drew closer to the shore, he heard Hoichi's inspired biwa playing. He followed the noise and found the blind minstrel sitting in the middle of the cemetery singing *The Tale of the Heike*. The servant grabbed Hoichi and pleaded for him to return to the temple; he told the singer he was bewitched and sitting in the cemetery where the Heike emperor, his grandmother, and military commanders were buried. The servant said they were surrounded by hundreds of demons. After much protest, Hoichi had no choice but to be dragged back. When they returned to the temple, Hoichi told the old priest everything that had happened.

The priest was frightened for his young friend, and he told Hoichi that if he returned the third night, he would be devoured by demons for all eternity. The priest also knew they could not stand against this spirit warrior, but he did have a plan. He wrote scripture all over the body of Hoichi and told him this would make him invisible to the ghostly samurai so long as he stayed perfectly still. That night at midnight, the samurai came again, saw Hoichi's biwa, but not the minstrel. He did, however, see two ears which had no writing on them at all. The samurai grabbed Hoichi's ears and tore them off so he could follow his lord's orders and bring back the only part of Hoichi he could find.

With the spell broken, the now disfigured Hoichi became a very soughtafter performer who became wealthy and famous for his telling of *The Tale of the Heike*.

The Akama-jingu Temple is still standing today and is a popular tourist destination in the industrial town of Shimonoseki, whose coast was the site of Dan-no-Ura.

# Part II

Ottoman War

(1356–1699)

# 2

# BRAN CASTLE

**War:** Ottoman Wars (1356–1683)
**Location:** Bran, Romania
**Participants:** Vlad "Vlad the Impaler" Tepes and the armies of Wallachia against the Ottoman Empire

*How blessed are some people, whose lives have no fears, no dreads, to whom sleep is a blessing that comes nightly, and brings nothing but sweet dreams.*

—From *Dracula*, by Bram Stoker

In the Romanian village of Bran, about 15 miles southwest of Brasov in the Carpathian Mountains, lies Bran Castle. Built in 1377 to protect the city of Brasov from invading Turks, the castle is more commonly referred to as "Dracula's Castle" because it is believed to have been the setting for Bram Stoker's gothic tale, *Dracula*. Though he never owned or lived at the castle, it is believed that Prince Vlad Tepes a.k.a. "Vlad the Impaler," son of Vlad Dracul ("Dracul" meaning "Devil"), once stayed here during an Ottoman siege.

*istockphoto.com/Mihai Zaharie*

Vlad Tepes was a knight of the Dragon Order—an order created by the Holy Roman Emperor Sigismund as an alliance of armies and warlords who would band together to fight the Turks. After the death of his father, Vlad took the moniker "Draculea" or "Draculya" or "The Devil's Son." He's now best known as the historical figure Bram Stoker used to create the Dracula character. But the real Draculya may have been more fierce and bloodthirsty than what Stoker concocted. Vlad's legend began in the Ottoman Wars in southeastern Europe.

It is difficult to put a date on the Ottoman Wars. The rise of the Ottoman Empire began in 1299 in the region of modern-day Turkey. During the 14th century, the Turks moved to expand their empire into central Europe and parts of the Middle East. One could place the start of the Ottoman Wars around 1356 when the Turks struck a blow against the weakening Byzantine Empire. Though the historians consider the end of the Ottoman Empire to be 1922, one could argue that the fighting that began around 1356 has never ended in the region that we call the Balkans today.

Between 1456 and 1462, Vlad Tepes was the strict ruler of Wallachia (modern-day southern Romania). To his credit, Vlad increased trade and the strength of his army, and he gave the most severe punishments for even the most petty of offenses so there was virtually no crime under his rule due to his people living in such ever-present fear. According to one folklore account, a cup made of gold leaf was left by a water well at a crossing in the road. No one dared touch it. When a woman discovered the cup missing one day, she knew Vlad Tepes was dead and wept because crime was going to return to the region. According to his legend, Draculya was ruthless against anyone who stood against him, and his infamy grew in his battles against the Turks. Though not the only military leader to incorporate this practice, Vlad was known to impale his captives on long spears—many times while they were still alive. Dying in this way could sometimes take hours if one was unlucky.

The legend of Draculya's battle practices spread. In his wake, Vlad left thousands of his fallen enemies on spears for all to see. He was also said to drink the blood of his enemy—a practice that furthered his savage reputation and instilled fear in the region. If you were a Turkish army facing Vlad Tepes, you knew what fate held for you if you succumbed in battle. Draculya's reputation served him well.

Soon, even Draculya's own countrymen feared him, and the Hungarian king had Vlad arrested and imprisoned in Visigrad Castle north of Budapest. But the imprisonment didn't last long because the Turks were rising up again and the King of Hungary had no greater weapon than Vlad Tepes. Vlad returned to Wallachia between 1476 and 1477 to lead his armies again, but the Turks came in such numbers that Wallachia fell and Vlad Tepes with it. Who killed Vlad, be it his own men, his enemy, or some accident in battle, will never be known. He was said to be buried in Snagov, north of Bucharest. A monastery sits on his tomb, but during an excavation, no body was found—further adding the mystery to his legend.

Bran Castle may still be home to some of the many tortured souls who died at Vlad's hand. In the courtyard, there is a fountain that conceals a hidden tunnel some 164 feet (50 meters) below the surface. Guests who know where to look and listen have claimed to have heard moans coming from within the tunnel. But victims aren't the only spirits said to haunt the castle. Many believe Vlad himself still passes through the castle and its grounds. He seems to be most active in the chamber he once used. People have photographed strange, glowing mists and light streaks within his room.

# Part III

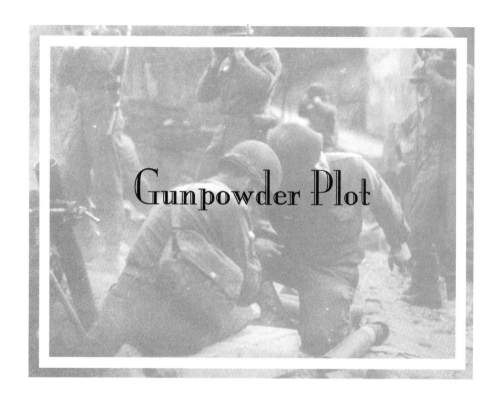

Gunpowder Plot

(1605)

# 3

# GUY FAWKES

**War:** The Gunpowder Plot (1605)
**Date:** November 5, 1605
**Location:** London, England
**Lived:** April 14, 1570 to January 31, 1606

*A desperate disease requires a dangerous remedy.*

—Guy Fawkes

What could be more dangerous than trying to blow up your country's king and everyone in its government? Only one thing: getting caught, facing the gallows, and being drawn and quartered.

The story of the Gunpowder Plot is as infamous today as the man tapped to carry out the deed. Guy Fawkes was an English soldier, a siegecraft expert, and a Roman Catholic who wanted to see the reign of King James I come to an end. To ensure a total overthrow of British government, Fawkes also wanted to eliminate all of the members of both houses of Parliament. The result, of course, would be anarchy—anarchy that Fawkes and his band hoped to quickly replace with a Roman Catholic monarch.

The problems for Roman Catholics in England began in 1563 with the second Act of Supremacy, which stated that England's monarch was not only the supreme ruler of the country, but also the Supreme Governor of the Church, and to hold a differing view was punishable by death. Catholics were forced to practice their faith in secret, priests were smuggled into the country, and mass was held in hidden rooms and private homes away from watchful eyes. As the 16th century waned, the British government was no longer turning a blind eye to Catholics practicing their religion.

King James I ascended to the throne of England in 1603 and set about standardizing the Bible and enforcing older laws regarding his theocratic position. The king's views on religious and legal issues led to multiple assassination attempts, but the Gunpowder Plot was the most significant.

In May of 1604, Robert Catesby, Thomas Percy, John Wright, and Robert Wintour concocted the Gunpowder Plot. Soon, seven others joined in the conspiracy: John Grant, Ambrose Rokewood, Robert Keyes, Sir Everard Digby, Francis Tresham, Thomas Bates (Robert Catesby's servant), and Guy Fawkes. The group rented a house near Westminster Palace and began tunneling their way toward the grand edifice. After almost a year of digging, it was clear to the men that the tunnel idea was easier conceived than executed. But the group caught a break in March of 1605 when Thomas Percy's Royal Court connections enabled him to rent a cellar directly below the House of Lords. They filled the vault with 36 barrels of gunpowder and then stacked firewood over the barrels to conceal them; then the waiting began. Summer turned to fall and the gunpowder secret remained safe. The plotters waited for their chance to take out the king and Parliament. That opportunity would come on November 5, 1605—the opening of Westminster Palace with King James I, the House of Lords, and the House of Commons all in attendance for the first time under the new roof. Among the pomp and circumstance, Guy Fawkes also wanted fire and blood. His job was to sneak into their cellar, light the fuse, and run for his life before the entire building was blown to bits.

On October 26, just days before the Gunpowder Plot was to be executed, an anonymous letter tipped off Parliament that treachery was afoot. It is believed that Francis Tresham sent the following letter to his Catholic relative, Lord Monteagle, in an effort to spare Catholic lives. The unsigned letter read:

*My lord, out of the love I bear to some of your friends, I have a care for your preservation. Therefore I would advise you, as you tender your life, to devise some excuse to shift of your attendance of this Parliament, for God and man hath concurred to punish the wickedness of this time. And think not slightly of this adver- tisement but retire yourself into your country, where you may expect the event in safety, for though there be no appearance of any stir, yet I say they shall receive a terrible blow, the Parliament, and yet they shall not see who hurts them. This counsel is not to be contemned, because it may do you good and can do you know harm, for the danger is past as soon as you have burnt the latter: and I hope God will give you the grace to make good use of it, to whose holy protection I commend you.*

Lord Monteagle passed the note to the Earl of Salisbury and the Secretary of State, who sent guards to the scene to arrest those found to be involved. Guy Fawkes was nabbed outside of the rented house.

Fawkes was tortured into revealing some of the other conspirators and he was then put through the formality of a trial. On January 31, 1606, Guy Fawkes, Robert Wintour, and several others who were implicated in the plot were taken to Old Palace Yard in front of the House of Parliament for a gruesome death. There is no crime more egregious than treason, and no penalty was worse than what they were about to receive. Fawkes and the others were to be dragged through the streets on hurdles to the site of their execution, hanged (not so their neck snaps, but almost to the point of suffocation), then taken down to be castrated, disemboweled, and cut into quarters.

Today Guy Fawkes is remembered throughout England, with his own holiday on November 5, and many know the popular nursery rhyme:

*Remember, remember the fifth of November*
*The gunpowder treason and plot.*
*I see no reason why gunpowder treason*
*Should ever be forgot.*
*Guy Fawkes, 'twas his intent*
*To blow up king and parliament.*

*Three score barrels were laid below*
*To prove old England's overthrow.*
*By God's mercy he was catched*
*With a dark lantern and lighted match.*
*Holler boys, holler boys, let the bells ring*
*Holler boys, holler boys, God save the King.*

Guy Fawkes is one of English history's wonderful villains. Each November 5th throughout Britain, the capture of Guy Fawkes is celebrated with fireworks displays and bonfires. Effigies of Fawkes are created and children cart them around from door-to-door during the day so they can collect pennies to buy fireworks. That evening, the Guy Fawkes effigies are burned.

A second tradition attached to Guy Fawkes involves the monarch's annual visit to Parliament. Ever since the Gunpowder Plot, the reigning king or queen comes to Parliament once a year for the State Opening of Parliament. Before the opening, the Yeomen of the Guard search the cellars of Westminster for signs of sabotage. Of course considering modern security measures, no one expects the search to yield anything, but the tradition is still carried out.

Generations of Brits have been raised celebrating the destruction of their country's most notorious traitor. This practice has burned into the British collective psyches what England does with its enemies from within. Who knows how many would-be plotters this holiday has deterred from ever attempting an overthrow of their government.

The Halloween/trick-or-treating/ghostly tradition is a relatively modern phenomenon in Britain. With Guy Fawkes' day less than a week after Halloween, some are starting to draw some supernatural conclusions that Guy Fawkes may still be around. Because Fawkes is remembered so prominently each year, perhaps there may be something to the ghostly claims that have been building.

In the autumn of 2005, medium Derek Acorah, best known as the psychic on the television show *Most Haunted*, filmed a television special called "Derek Acorah's Quest for Guy Fawkes." At the Old Palace Yard where the body of Guy Fawkes was hung, drawn, and quartered, Acorah claimed Guy Fawkes came through to him. "I was blown away when he came through to me," Acorah said in a November 3, 2005, *Liverpool Echo* interview. "While expressing himself through me, Guy Fawkes revealed that the one who betrayed him to the king was not Francis Tresham as was previously believed. In fact, it was someone very close to Fawkes: one of his plotters."

It's unlikely that historians will ever change the history books on the word of a psychic, but the experiences of Derek Acorah, the way Guy Fawkes is remembered, and an increasing awareness of the supernatural may lead others to start seeking and finding the ghost of the infamous Guy Fawkes.

# *Part IV*

British Civil War

(1642–1660)

# 4

# EDGEHILL BATTLEFIELD

**War:** British Civil War (1642–1660)
**Date of battle:** October 23, 1642
**Location:** Warwickshire, England
**Participants:** The Earl of Essex and roughly 14,000 of his Roundheads against King Charles's Royalist army, also about 14,000 strong
**Casualties:** Over 3,000

Every war has that defining moment where tensions boil over, the time for talk ends, and forces clash on the battlefield. Every war has its first battle, and the British Civil War has Edgehill. Located in central England, Edgehill wasn't the predetermined site for the first battle—it didn't hold much military significance—but it was a hill, and in hand-to-hand combat, one prefers to be uphill rather than down. This clash led to a centuries-old ghostly legend in the hills and skies of Warwickshire.

The two factions fighting in the British Civil War were the Royalists who supported their monarch, King Charles I (1600–1649), and the Roundheads, who wanted to abolish the monarchy and move to a representative and more democratic government.

King Charles was devoted to the Anglican Church and believed his kingship to be divinely appointed. When Charles's older brother, Prince Henry, died when Charles was 12 years old, it was God who made the decision that Charles would be king. In 1625, Charles took the throne.

King Charles needed money to pursue his war policies. He needed to build up his navy for defense and to fund the Duke of Buckingham who waged battles against France and Spain and their Catholic rulers. The move made Buckingham unpopular with the Parliament, who wanted to impeach him. To protect his subject, King Charles abolished the Parliament—a move that also meant forfeiting the tax revenue that came with the organization. When he needed money again, Charles reestablished another Parliament, which made legal moves to defend against the king's arbitrary and abusive use of power. King Charles was forced to accept the proposal because he felt he would get subsidies from the Parliament to pursue his war endeavors. Plus, Charles also had no intention of following the proposal.

The Duke of Buckingham was assassinated in 1628. It seemed as though the legal means of removing the Duke were waved off by Buckingham's supportive king, so some took matters into their own hands. King Charles was infuriated by the murder and dismissed the Parliament once again in 1629, beginning a period known as the "Eleven Year Tyranny."

In some respects, the Monarch was successful. He established trade ties with his former enemies, France and Spain, and he stabilized his economy, enabling him to commission works of art and build his Royal Navy. But the lack of a Parliament meant the king had to raise money by highly unpopular means such as forced loans, selling commercial enterprises, and his most loathsome policy of "ship money," which required coastal towns with ports to completely fund the Royal Navy ships' upkeep. In 1640, Charles was obliged to reinstate Parliament again so he could tax his people and they could believe they had representation in their rule.

Given King Charles's history of ignoring or dismissing Parliament whenever he disagreed with them, some countrymen grew restless knowing that they had no voice in government at all. During 1642, both the king and the Parliament were making legal moves to control the armed forces in an effort to move the country closer to a democracy. The king tried to have the five loudest voices of his Parliamentary opposition arrested, and both sides began to look to their countrymen for support in the growing conflict. King Charles pleaded that England needed a Monarch and he was in fact divinely appointed; the Parliament spoke of a government that catered to the needs of its people—where its citizens had some voice. On August 22, 1642, the argument came to a head. King Charles raised the royal battle flag over Nottingham Castle and declared war against Parliament. He called all loyal subjects to arms.

The king gathered Royalists from Yorkshire, Staffordshire, and Lincolnshire and seized all the weapons they could in their region, then moved west to Cheshire, then south to Shrewsbury in an effort to collect more troops and supplies. The call to arms yielded less than they expected, but enough to mount a formidable force. Parliament's army of Roundheads—initially a derogatory term derived for their short hair—was led by Robert Devereux, the Earl of Essex who left London and marched north to Northampton to gather his own forces. Essex intended to move his men against the king in Nottingham but soon found out that the king's army was on the move. Essex learned the king had moved into Wales so he headed west to Worcester, just inside the Welsh border. Both sides felt there would be a single decisive battle that would end the war, and each force was prowling the countryside, seeking a place where they could take up an advantageous position.

On October 12, 1642, King Charles and his army left Shrewsbury with the intention of marching south to London, and a week later Essex and his troops left Worcester on a hunt for the king. On October 22, Essex was only seven miles from the king's army. When the Royalist officers learned of their enemy's position, they advised the king not to continue toward London because they could not fight on two opposite fronts effectively, so King Charles's army made for the highest ridge of Edgehill and waited for Essex to approach.

Essex saw the Royalist position and knew there would be no point in assailing the steep slopes of the hill, so he moved his forces into the plain below and waited. The Royalists followed suit and moved their forces further down to engage their enemy, removing all doubt that there was going to, indeed, be a battle in Edgehill.

For the rest of the afternoon the forces clashed. The Parliament army had traitors in their midst, and Royalist officers knew it. During the initial charge of Prince Rupert and his Royalist cavalry toward the Parliament army's left wing, Sir Faithful Fortescue's Parliamentary troop spun around to fight alongside the Royalists against their former comrades. Retreats, regroups, and charges were the order of the afternoon, and, by nightfall, both armies were exhausted and withdrew. Each army claimed victory, though neither side overtook the other's position and thousands from both sides lay dead or wounded on the field; their bodies were soon looted for clothes, money, and anything else of value.

Though there was no apparent winner, the Royalist army still had a clear road to London, so, tactically, they could be declared the victor.

The British Civil War had begun, blood had been shed, and the fight toward a more representative government was on.

The ghostly accounts at Edgehill began soon after the battle. Shepherds tending to their flocks in the region claimed to hear the sound of drums, then a cacophony of battle, and the groans of the dying. They said they witnessed a spectral replay of the battle on the ground, and then again in the sky. The hallowed and haunted battlefield's reputation took its place in local lore and was so prominent that printer Thomas Jackson published some of the many stories in 1643, just a year after the battle. King Charles was intrigued when he heard some of the tales, and he sent some of his officers to investigate. The legend says the officers came to the site and witnessed the gruesome vision of the battle being replayed again; they even claimed to witness men they knew fighting and dying again in the phantom battle.

Throughout the centuries, the sightings of the battle have decreased, but the site is still considered to be among England's most-haunted locations because, at this point, the legend of the ghosts have eclipsed the legends of the battle. Today many still report strange streaks of light and the sounds of clanking armor, which they attribute to the ghosts of the Edgehill battle.

# 5

# LION HOTEL

**War:** British Civil War (1642–1660)
**Location:** Shrewsbury, England

Ghosts of soldiers aren't just confined to battlefields and boats. Sometimes they roam old houses, government buildings, and even English pubs. Such is the case with the Lion Hotel in Shrewsbury, England. Built in the early 17th century, the hotel boasts notable past guests such as Charles Dickens, King William IV, and Madame Tussaud. Similar to many respectable old buildings, it also houses a ghost or two, but the legend of a British soldier's ghost said to haunt the pub is what caught my attention.

For help with the ghosts of the Lion Hotel, I spoke with Stuart Edmunds, a local paranormal investigator who first visited the building for an article he wrote for the BBC on the hauntings there. Edmunds has been interested in researching the paranormal since his university days when he studied filmmaking. He found his field of study gave him an easy entrée into certain haunted locations that welcomed a student endorsed by a university. As it is for many paranormal investigators, receiving permission to get inside can be the biggest challenge.

Stuart Edmunds was drawn to the Lion Hotel because a friend who worked there had told him about their ghosts. The Lion was interesting to him because it's an obscure locale as far as English haunts go—a great benefit to those who study the paranormal. When too many people know about specific phenomena at a location, it can taint the results. For example, at the Tower of London, the headless ghost of Queen Anne Boleyn, one of King Henry VIII's wives, is so well-known that she's made it into folk songs: "With her head tucked underneath her arm/She walks the Bloody Tower! With her head tucked underneath her arm/At the Midnight hour." When visitors go to the Tower of London knowing this bit of lore, they are influenced by it. A shadow may dart by (even a perfectly natural one) and some may leap to the conclusion that it's Anne Boleyn. At the Lion Hotel, we don't have this problem because its ghosts are not that well-known, and the Lion doesn't promote a haunted reputation to help get curiosity seekers in the door. Edmunds first investigated the hotel in the spring of 2005.

"They were actually welcoming at the hotel, which is quite a rarity," Edmunds said. "When you're trying to do an investigation, you don't usually get welcomed in too many places. But they were quite keen to see what we could capture."

For equipment, Stuart brought along video cameras with night vision (or near-infrared) capabilities, thermometers, an Electromagnetic Field or EMF meter, and some coins for trigger objects. I notice that paranormal investigators in the United Kingdom tend to use trigger objects more than their North American counterparts. The concept behind trigger objects is to place something such as a coin on a lined piece of paper or perhaps on a bed of flour or other fine powder and leave this setup in an area or room with reported supernatural activity. If you have sealed the room correctly, when the investigator returns he or she will be able to see if these objects have moved because there will be a disturbance in the flour or the coins will have crossed lines on the paper. It's low-tech, super-inexpensive, and definitely old-school ghost hunting.

What makes this hotel a military site? It turns out that in no less than three wars there were soldiers stationed at the Lion: the British Civil War (1642–1660), World War I (1914–1919), and World War II (1939–1945). It has also been said that the Lion Hotel was used to treat the wounded during the British Civil War. Could one of these soldiers still be there today?

"The intention of the night investigation was to spend as much time in the cellar as possible because we were told the cellar is where people were the most terrified and thought there were things going on," Edmunds said. "But it was actually in the Tudor Bar that we found something."

The Tudor Bar is a small lounge next to the main reception area of the hotel. Edmunds had learned that one of the cleaning crew had an experience in there early one morning in the late 1990s. The woman glanced through the glass partition that separates the bar from the lobby and saw what she described as a soldier who looked like he had just come from battle. "We're assuming it's the ghost of a possible Redcoat from Oliver Cromwell's army," Edmunds said. "There were two or three battles around Shrewsbury as well, so that all tied in." During the British Civil War, Oliver Cromwell led a cavalry troop against King Charles's Royalist army. Cromwell took a new approach to recruiting his officers. He promoted his men based on merit instead of how much money they had or their social standing. Cromwell once wrote: "I would rather have a plain russet-coated captain who knows what he fights for and loves what he knows than that which you call a gentleman and is nothing else." It may have been one of Cromwell's men who spent some time convalessing at the Lion Hotel in the days of the Civil War.

During his investigation, Edmund experienced various anomalies including cold spots, orbs, or semi-translucent balls of light, on some of the photographs he took. While using the night vision feature on his video camera in the bar area, he says he caught strange wisps of light drifting past the camera that would then be accompanied by a cold spot. The most intriguing and unexplainable event of the investigation also occurred in the pub area. One of the female members of his team is a sensitive to the paranormal, meaning she can often pick up on feelings and images that other people can't. "She saw someone out of the corner of her eye sit in a particular chair at the bar," Edmunds said. "She told me she had just seen somebody in the corner sit on a stool. I started taking lots of random still photos, and we caught these really strange bright lights hovering above the stool so I walked over and checked it out. When this happened, you could actually hear it. The stool had thick leather, and as soon as you sit up off the leather, it makes a noise that's quite unmistakable. We heard that noise as if somebody had just gotten up off the stool. I went over and got a photo of it."

Edmunds and his team watched as indents in the seat slowly disappeared over the span of about 10 seconds—just as thick leather seats do when someone gets off of them. He caught a picture of the seat.

*Could this be the print of a ghost who just stood up at the Lion Hotel?*
*Photo by Stuart Edmunds*

"It was my intention to stay awake all night and try and catch something to see if it was a cycle where you see the ghost at the same time in the same place every week or every day," Edmunds said. A common theory with ghosts is that some are residual hauntings—meaning these apparitions show up at the same time and place at regular intervals because they aren't really there. They were there at one point in time and whatever happened in the location has left kind of a psychic impression that replays itself like a movie.

The soldier's ghost isn't the only spirit said to be haunting the old hotel. A gray lady has been spotted floating past the Tapestry Lounge, another female spirit has been experienced in the cellar, and a third woman ghost has been reported walking the balcony in the ballroom like she was looking for someone or something. But the Tudor Bar seems to be reserved for the ghost of a soldier who may just be waiting for one last round of drinks before he hits the road.

# 6

# LORD CAPEL AND
# CASSIOBURY PARK

**War:** British Civil War
**Location:** Watford, England
**Casualties:** 2

March 9 and July 13 are two important dates at Cassiobury Park in Watford, England, because on these days each year, two respective ghosts are said to wander through the park. To discover who these people were, we'll need to travel back to a time just before the British Civil War.

In 1627, Elizabeth Morrison married Arthur Lord Capel of Hadham, at which time a grand mansion, whose construction was started by Elizabeth's grandfather Sir Richard Morrison in 1546 and completed by her father Sir Charles Morrison in 1556, passed into the Capel family. This was a time period where lineage, pedigree, and the family one married into meant everything.

Cassiobury House had 84 rooms, a gallery, stables, a dairy, and a brewhouse and was set in the lush gardens of Cassiobury Park. Arthur Lord Capel and his family moved in and the estate became his seat of power. Capel was Lord of the Manor and a member of Parliament for Hertfordshire. Though he was a staunch Royalist, he was also rather outspoken against King Charles in the time leading up to the British Civil War.

For more insight on Cassiobury Park, its history, and its ghosts, I spoke with Sarah Priestly, the Heritage Officer at the Watford Museum. Priestly has worked at the museum since 2000 and considering her university degree in history and her teaching qualifications, she's well-suited to study and explore the history and lore of Watford. She also happens to know a thing or two about their ghosts. "I do quite a lot of ghost storytelling at the museum," Priestly said. "We encourage it. Because quite often even if they're legends and we don't know the facts exactly, there's a lot of historical information there. Some of the legends that we have tell you an awful lot about the age. They tell you a lot about the people. A lot of children would find the Civil War a very dry subject, but if you add a beheaded ghost into it, then it helps them remember it. We're not afraid to confront our ghosts—maybe our demons, but not our ghosts."

Priestly talked about the kind of man Arthur Lord Capel was, and how he felt King Charles needed to change his ways, accept the input of Parliament, and go a little easier on the many English people who didn't accept the king's religious dictate. Though Capel felt change was necessary, he didn't want to see the issue come to war. But in October of 1642, the inevitable happened and the first shots were fired. "Suddenly Arthur Lord Capel was surrounded by all of this turmoil, and that's really not what he wanted," Priestly said. "He wanted the king to change, but he didn't want to go without a king. You could say that the king had no greater ally and no more committed supporter. Even when the king had been imprisoned, Arthur continued on."

After a string of Royalist army defeats, things weren't looking good for King Charles. After narrowly escaping the Siege of Oxford in April of 1646, the king put himself in the care of the Scottish Presbyterian army, who held him until an agreement was reached with Parliament. In 1647 King Charles was imprisoned at Holdenby House in Northamptonshire.

But through the arrests and the impending defeat of the Royalists, Arthur Lord Capel continued his support for the crown through Parliament—a move that would cost him dearly. Capel was arrested for high treason against Parliament and was sent to the Tower of London to await his fate.

On January 30, 1649, King Charles was beheaded. Over the next few weeks, Arthur Lord Capel learned he was to receive the same treatment as his king. "His dying wish was that his heart be taken from his body and placed in a silver case at the foot of the king," Priestly said. "It was a very grand gesture. It was very much the kind of person he was."

Capel's heart was removed and placed in a box after his execution on March 9, 1649. And because of his family's political influence, Parliament allowed them to keep possession of Cassiobury House and their estate, meaning Capel's son, also named Arthur, could inherit everything.

"It was about 60 years later that someone within the Cassiobury household found the box and opened it," Priestly said. "And there inside was a slightly less rounded heart than it started off as. It was quite gruesome. It never made it to the king."

When Charles II came to the throne of England and restored the monarchy, he rewarded those who supported the crown. Arthur Lord Capel's son was awarded the title of Earl of Essex—a designation that would stay in his family even though the second Arthur Capel would grow up to be implicated in a plot to overthrow King Charles II. In 1683 he was imprisoned at the Tower of London, was held in the same cell as his father, and accused of the same crime: high treason. Arthur Capel, Earl of Essex, was found with his throat slit on July 13, 1683, before his accusers had the opportunity to find him guilty. Was he murdered or did he commit suicide as a noble gesture to his family? No matter the cause, because he was dead, there would be no trial, and his title and estate would be allowed to stay in his family.

Today, both Arthur Lord Capels are said to haunt Cassiobury Park. The first Lord Capel's headless ghost is said to wander the grounds of the park on the anniversary of his death every March 9. And his son Arthur Junior's ghost is believed to come through the park on horseback on the anniversary of his death every July 13. These ghosts are still discussed in the ghost tours offered by the Watford Museum, and they're whispered about by children who enjoy a good scare. But how far back does this ghostlore go? "The legends go back for hundreds of years," Priestly said. "In fact, there is evidence in diaries from Cassiobury dating back to October 1841 from one of the teenage girls that lived in the house who was the daughter of the Earls. She wrote in her diary about listening to her grandmamma telling ghost stories at Cassiobury House. These are stories that have been passed on from generation to generation. But I don't know anyone who's actually seen the ghost. It's now part of history in its own right."

Folklore is oral tradition, it's an intimate form of communication, and it's a legitimate form of sharing information. Folklore obviously plays a significant role in the study of ghosts—it serves as a starting point and begs us to dig deeper. Folklore is a story that has been passed around so much that the source may be long gone, yet everyone seems to know the basic story. Perhaps some embellishments came in along the way, but some basis in fact remains—there's a reason the story started in the first place.

I spoke with Dr. Michael Bell, an author and lecturer who has his Ph.D. in folklore, about the nature of the legends like those at Cassiobury Park. "Legends take shape in conversation when someone tells about something he heard or experienced that seems worth passing along to others," Dr. Bell said. "If the narrative is interesting or seems worth repeating, then others who heard it will keep telling it. As the story becomes part of oral tradition, it is altered by people—both purposefully as well as unintentionally—and the variation that is a hallmark of legends (and all folklore, for that matter) becomes evident. Legends and belief are inextricably intertwined. For example, if a story is totally believable or unbelievable, its chances of becoming a legend are very small."

The legends at Cassiobury Park are mentioned in a diary dating back to 1841, so we know the ghosts here go back at least that far. We also know that the first Arthur Lord Capel was indeed beheaded, and his son was found dead in the Tower of London. There is a basis in fact and in history to support the supernatural claims. These two men, a father and son, one who played a role in the Civil War and the other implicated in a treasonous plot to overthrow his king, survive to this day, even if only in ghostly form. Something unexplained happened here because we still talk about the ghosts and still remember the men behind them.

# *Part V*

American Revolution

# (1775–1783)

# 7

# BRIGADIER GENERAL "MAD ANTHONY" WAYNE

**Wars:** American Revolution (1775–1783)
Northwest Indian War (1785–1795)
**Notable battle:** Stony Point, New York, July 16, 1779
**Lived:** January 1, 1745—December 15, 1796

*Yet the resources of this country are great and if councils will call them forth we may produce a conviction to the world that we deserve to be free—for my own part, I am such an enthusiast for independence that I would hesitate to enter heaven thro' the means of a secondary cause unless I had made the utmost exertions to merit it.*

—Gen. Anthony Wayne in a letter to Robert Morris,
October 26, 1781

For almost two centuries, the people who live in Pennsylvania have heard the lore of Mad Anthony Wayne, a ghostly Revolutionary War–era officer who has been seen all along Route 322—a 400-mile stretch of road that diagonally crosses the state from Erie in the northwest to just outside of Philadelphia in the southeastern part of the state. The legend says that every New Year's morning, the ghostly general rises from his grave in

Radnor, Pennsylvania, outside of Philadelphia, rides 400 miles to Erie, then returns. What's he looking for? His bones.

*Photo courtesy of the Library of Congress*

Anthony Wayne was born in Chester County in southeastern Pennsylvania. He was named after his grandfather, a soldier in the British army who had emigrated to America. The people and influences in Wayne's life read like a veritable who's who of America's founding fathers.

Wayne became a surveyor after studying in his uncle's private Philadelphia academy and was then sent by Benjamin Franklin to Nova Scotia to survey land there. After returning home, he became active in Chester County politics and served in the Pennsylvania legislature from 1774 to 1775 until the American Revolution stirred the winds of change in the new United States. Wayne raised his own militia and became a colonel in the Fourth Regiment of Pennsylvania.

Col. Wayne's regiment was part of the Continental Army's unsuccessful invasion of the Canadian provinces, during which time he was placed in charge of the troubled Fort Ticonderoga on Lake Champlain in upstate New York. His valor in battle earned the colonel a promotion to brigadier-general on February 21, 1777. During the winter 1777 and 1778, General Wayne was stationed at Valley Forge with General George Washington. The meeting would be important to Wayne's future military and political life, but it was a battle in July 1779 that would earn General Wayne his maniacal moniker "Mad Anthony."

At King's Ferry on the Hudson River in New York stood the imposing British fort Stony Point. The fort was a key position to the British because they could control the mighty Hudson River and stop war and troop ships from using the waterway to move inland. The fort was 150 feet high and stood perched on a rocky bluff on the western shore of the Hudson. Stony Point was surrounded by water on three sides and on the fourth side was a swamp. A significant number of cannons and more than 600 men (led by Lt. Col. Henry Johnson) were inside making the stronghold almost impenetrable. One would have to be mad to attempt an attack.

Gen. Wayne had a plan, and Gen. George Washington approved. Washington said in a letter that Wayne's secret plan should "be attempted by the Light Infantry only, which should march under cover of the night and with the utmost secrecy to the enemy's lines, securing every person they find to prevent discovery." On the evening of July 15, 1779, Gen. Wayne gathered 1,000 men and laid out his plan. Every soldier knew his task and where and when he should be on the hill.

As hundreds of American rebels crept up the hill, the British soldiers stirred and rained cannon and musket fire down in the dark. Gen. Wayne suffered a blow to his scalp and felt his own wet blood soaking his face. His knees were getting weaker, but he managed to scream at his men to press on. Wayne was helped to his feet by one of his men. "Help me into the fort," Gen. Wayne told him. "I mean to die at the head of my column." Through the mud, the sweat, and the blood, Wayne reached the top, and his determination and ferocity inspired his men around him. Soon American forces poured over the outer walls, swamping the fort in the middle where they met at the flagpole. The British Union Jack flag was lowered and the fort surrendered. In total, 63 Brits were killed in action and 543 were taken prisoner, compared with 15 Americans killed and 83 wounded. Wayne sent Gen. Washington a letter after the battle that read: "The fort and garrison with Lt. Col. Johnson are ours. Our officers and men behaved like men who are determined to be free." The legend of Mad Anthony Wayne was born, and forces on both sides of the conflict were stunned at the outcome.

Gen. Wayne was decorated for his valor and leadership in the battle. He led his forces in other battles and victories, though none were as brilliant as Stony Point. After the Americans had won their revolution, Gen. Wayne returned to Pennsylvania and resumed his political life. In 1785 he moved to Georgia with the intent to settle on the tract of land given to him by the state's government for his military service there.

Wayne became a congressman representing Georgia in 1791, but he lost his seat when a political rival sparked a debate over residency eligibility.

Wayne's military and political retirement would be short-lived, as Gen. George Washington called him into military service again. This time, Wayne was asked to lead the newly formed Legion of the United States forces in the Northwest Indian War—a conflict that wasn't going well for the United States. Many of the Indians had sided with the British during the Revolutionary War, and, once the British formally pulled out of the United States, it left their Native American allies in a bit of a military limbo save for a few British outposts in the western territory. Many Indians felt they were still at war and intended to defend their front and prevent the Americans from conquering the entire land mass out to the Pacific Ocean.

In 1793, along the Wabash River in Ohio, Gen. Wayne established Fort Recovery as a base to spearhead his operations. His labors turned the war effort around for the Americans. On August 20, 1794, the general commanded an assault on the Indian confederacy at the Battle of Fallen Timbers south of present-day Toledo, Ohio. The American victory ended the Northwest Indian War. The British ended their support and supply of Indian forces and surrendered the bases they had established in the northwestern territories.

On a trip to Pennsylvania from a military outpost in Detroit, Gen. Wayne developed gout and succumbed to the disease on December 15, 1796. He was buried at Presque Isle, which is modern-day Erie, Pennsylvania. But Mad Anthony Wayne's story doesn't end here.

Wayne's son, Isaac, wanted his father's remains to be buried in the family plot at St. David's Episcopal Church Cemetery in Radnor, Pennsylvania, outside of Philadelphia. Isaac sent word and then left for Erie to collect his father's remains. Unbeknownst to Isaac, local physician Dr. James Wallace boiled Gen. Wayne's remains to separate what was left of his flesh from his bones. The General's clothes and flesh were then reinterred under the blockhouse on Presque Isle. When Isaac arrived, he was given his father's bones.

The legend says that as Isaac traveled southeast along the route to Radnor, some of Mad Anthony's bones fell out of the wagon, and he's now scattered along what became U.S. Route 322. According to the lore, every year on his birthday, January 1, Mad Anthony rises from his grave and travels to Erie looking for his mortal remains and then returns to rest for another year.

# Part VI

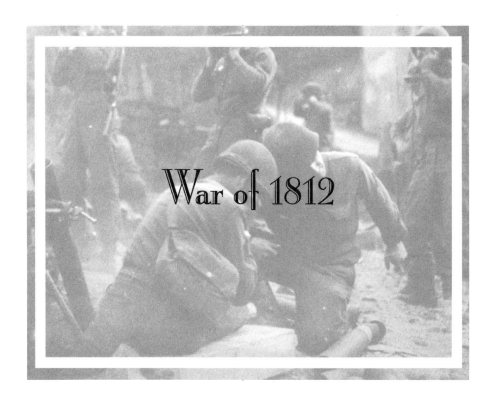

War of 1812

(1812–1814)

# 8

# FORT MEIGS

**War:** War of 1812 (1812–1814)
**Date of battle:** April 30–May 8 and July 21–28, 1813
**Location:** Perrysburg, Ohio
**Participants:** United States General William Henry Harrison against Tecumseh and his Indian forces and British General Henry A. Proctor
**Casualties:** 400–500 who died in the two battles, in skirmishes surrounding the fort, and from illnesses related to the living conditions

*Tell General Proctor that if he shall take the fort it will be under circumstances that will do him more honor than a thousand surrenders.*
—U.S. General William Henry Harrison in a note to British General Proctor, May 4, 1813

Fort Meigs marked a turning point in the War of 1812, a war that wasn't going well in the northwestern region of the United States at the time. America had been defeated in Dearborn, Mackinac, Detroit, and Frenchtown, and another rout could lead to the loss of the entire region. The stockades and forces at Fort Meigs held through two attacks and sieges, but not without its price. Today there are still echoes from those who fought. Some have claimed that even the spirits of Native Americans who lived here for centuries before the fort was built still roam the grounds. Many people today report strange glowing masses of light and even the apparitions of American soldiers, but there is an even higher rate of unexplained occurrences around blockhouse number three.

On January 22, 1813, General William Henry Harrison (a man who would go on to become the ninth president of the United States) and 900 of his men were fleeing Frenchtown (modern-day Monroe, Michigan) after a failed American offensive against British General Henry A. Proctor. Along the Raisin River in Frenchtown, U.S. Major General James Winchester let his guard down and didn't post enough sentries to watch the town at night. By morning, British cannon fire was raining down from all around and the Redcoats swarmed like angry hornets. Of Winchester's 960 men, over 300 were killed and 500 were captured, including Winchester himself, and the rest ran south to catch up with General Harrison's men. When the escapees caught up with Harrison, they were panicked and warned that an exaggeratedly immense British and Indian force was heading south to finish off any American troops in the area. Harrison's only choice was to give up Michigan territory and keep moving south to find a position where they stood a fighting chance.

When Harrison reached a hill on the banks of the Maumee River in northwest Ohio that evening, he ordered his 900 men to dig in—all the while checking over their shoulders to the north to watch for advancing British and Indian forces. The men dug and pick-axed through the cold weather without rest because if their enemy closed in, this could very well be the last stand for the northwestern United States. After almost two weeks had gone by and no enemy came, General Harrison figured a British attack wouldn't come until spring, so he set his men to building a more significant fort.

The site was ominous even before First Lieutenant Joseph Larwell helped Captain Charles Cratiot of the U.S. Engineers survey the encampment. During the building process, many artifacts were uncovered.

I spoke to John Kachuba, author of *Ghosthunting Ohio*, who researched the history and ghosts at Fort Meigs. "When they were building the fort, they were turning up bones left and right," Kachuba said. "There was a diary of a guy named Captain Daniel Cushing, and in his diary he says, 'Walking around this garrison on the earth that has been thrown up was like walking on the seashore upon muscle shells, only in this case, human bones.' As they were digging a trench in front of blockhouses number three and four, they came upon a pile of bones where they took out 25 skulls in one pit. They don't know for sure if it was a burial site or a massacre site, but it had been an Indian encampment for many years."

More American soldiers arrived from Kentucky and Virginia, bringing the garrison totals up to 1,800 men. When completed, the fort's log stockade enclosed 10 acres, seven two-level blockhouses, and five emplacements, or prepared cannon positions. They dug large earthen parapets on the riverside of the fort, offering protection from any attack that might come from the water. When the basic configuration was complete, General Harrison named the fort in honor of Ohio Governor Jonathan Meigs.

Gen. Harrison was promised 10,000 men for the Northwest army, but in the winter of 1813, he had roughly 6,000 who were spread along a 200-mile line front from Fort Meigs down through Indiana. On March 5, Gen. Harrison was called away to tend to his sick children, and while he was gone, the rank and file fell apart at the fort.

Brigadier General Joel Leftwich of the Virginia militia was left in charge of Fort Meigs with orders to continue its fortification. Instead, Leftwich allowed his men to use the timber for heating fuel. To make matters worse, Leftwich's troops' enlistment period ended April first, and his intention was to go home. Many other men at Fort Meigs also were scheduled to leave by the end of March, bringing the Fort Meigs force down to only 500. If the British attacked, the region would be lost.

General Harrison, upon hearing of the breakdown at the fort, left immediately to return. In under a week, Harrison had managed to scare up another 3,500 soldiers—some from his own Western line, but most from Governor Isaac Shelby of Kentucky who sent reinforcements.

Back in Michigan, General Proctor was also building a force of more than 2,200—about 1,000 British and Canadian militia and 1,200 Indian. On April 26, they set out for Fort Meigs. Two days later, they began to set up camp 2 miles from the fort.

General Harrison's scouts saw the British movement and reported in. Harrison ordered the base to be readied for defense as British scouts watched unabashedly from the opposite side of the Maumee River. Harrison then ordered Capt. Eleazor Darby Wood to dig trenches and set up earthen blockades. Wood first ordered his troops to set up rows of tents along the river banks to conceal what they were doing—a move that would soon pay off.

On April 30, a British gunboat drifted down the Maumee and fired at Fort Meigs but it achieved little. Around 11 the next morning, General Proctor opened up his cannon artillery on the Americans inside the fort. Once the first salvo was cleared away, Harrison ordered the blockade of tents removed, which revealed his "grand traverse" to the British—a 12-foot-high, 300-yard-long mound of dirt shielding the American supplies and troops. Firing cannon balls at this mound was about as much use as punching a giant sponge.

General Proctor's hope for a fast surrender was quickly dashed. General Harrison gave the order to his quartermaster: "Sir, go and nail a flag on every battery where they shall wave as long as an enemy is in view." Until late that night the British fired heavy and light rounds at the fort, and by midnight only two Americans were dead and four injured, but a steady rain was turning everything to mud, including the giant traverse dug just a few days prior.

May 2 saw an all-day assault from Proctor and the British and Indian forces. Fort Meigs returned fire sparingly, considering their supplies of ammunition. General Harrison offered the reward of a gill (about 4 ounces) of whiskey for every 6-pound British cannonball his men could recover for firing back. The more whiskey the men received, the braver they became at facing the British gunfire. More than 1,000 cannon balls were recovered.

For two more days, the British battering continued until a scout arrived informing Harrison that reinforcements were only 45 miles away. Gen. Harrison devised a plan to counterattack the British from Fort Meigs while the reinforcements flanked the British troops on the opposite side of the river and American gunboats could drift in and have their pick of targets.

The plan came together, and American forces chased the Indians through the woods all the way back to the British camp two miles away. The reinforcements successfully took out many of the British cannon batteries on the opposite shore of the Maumee, and the British retreated to their own camp to take up defensive positions. Of the 846 men under Colonel Dudley who chased the Indians back to the British base camp, only 170 made it back to Fort Meigs. The American rout was successful in securing their fort, but disastrous considering the losses that could have been avoided had the men stopped once the British fled their siege. Harrison sent out men from the fort to help break the Redcoat defensive lines that were forming during their retreat. The British came back for a few more cannon attacks on Fort Meigs in the coming days, but when Harrison returned fire with great numbers and fury on May 8, Proctor conceded that the fort would not be his and pulled out.

Tecumseh was appalled at the leadership and performance of Proctor during the battle and made this thoughts clear to the General. However, the two agreed to a return to the Maumee River on July 21, this time with greater numbers than the first siege. They devised a plan to draw the American army out of the fort and then ambush them, but General Harrison didn't fall for it. On July 28, Proctor, the British, and the Indian forces gave up their hopes of capturing Fort Meigs and moved 30 miles east to the American Fort Stephenson, where their charge was also costly and ineffective in driving the Americans out. Proctor dragged his men back to Michigan.

The past is still alive at Fort Meigs in many ways. The site offers regular tours from volunteers in period dress, and many have reported experiences spanning the supernatural spectrum from simple uneasy feelings to seeing strange balls of light and even recognizable apparitions.

John Destatte is a 52-year-old history buff who has been volunteering at Fort Meigs since the early 1990s. He grew up in the area, and though he hasn't seen the ghosts himself, he's heard many reports from people who have.

"Blockhouse number three always seems to be a place where a lot of people say they see things," Destatte said. "I'm one of the resident skeptics. I don't necessarily believe in these things, but it's food for thought when you hear a number of people repeatedly give the same accounts and the same stories, and you say well, maybe there is something to this.

"Blockhouse number three was destroyed during the first battle at the fort, essentially from artillery fire from across the river. During the original construction, there was found to be many remains of Native Americans who are buried on that site, which is natural because it's a nice prominent point looking over the river. A lot of people say they feel an Indian presence there, or they seem to see some sort of Indian spirit. Then there's the other people who say they see a woman and child looking out of the upstairs of the blockhouse."

"Was there any record of a woman and child there?" I asked.

"It doesn't really tie into anything we've ever come across. Blockhouses were not used for people to stay in. We don't know of anything that would indicate why people would see that apparition. But those two things always seem to be associated with blockhouse number three. We know that there were probably some refugees from the local area that might have taken shelter here. Some of them were probably from Frenchtown, which is present-day Monroe, Michigan, and there are some references to women at the camp, but there really isn't much to go by."

Destatte explained how many of the Perrysburg locals will walk around the fort in the evenings, walking their dogs, or just going for a stroll. Some of these locals have contacted the fort to ask some peculiar questions. "Off the east end of the fort there was a local kid hanging out. His parents called a couple days after he was up there and asked what was going on this last weekend. And I said, 'Well, there wasn't anything going on. We didn't have any events or anything, why?' And he said his son was up there and he heard drums and music and horses, men marching over where the cemetery is. And he was wondering if we were having a reenactment up there.

"That was a new story, I never heard that before, but when you stop and think about it, it makes sense because that's exactly where Miller's charge was. And he probably would've heard men marching, and the drums and fifes and horses because they were right in the area where this kid said he heard all of the noise."

On May 5, Colonel John Miller and 19th U.S. Infantry led a sortie consisting of 350 men from seven companies against the British and Indian battery in the ravine on the east end of Fort Meigs. The men charged in full view of their enemy. Indian snipers fired at them from the tree line and British soldiers fired back head-on. By noon, Miller accomplished his goal of spiking the nearby British cannons and he managed to capture 42 prisoners in the charge.

Another hot spot for sightings at Fort Meigs are the giant earthen traverses. During the sieges, some brave (and probably a little bit crazy) men from the fort would stand on the traverses and watch the British artillery shots launch from across the river. The spotters would call out if they felt the shell was going to fly over the fort, or announce where they thought it might land inside—giving the American forces a second or two to take cover.

On May 5, when U.S. General Green Clay and his 1,200 reinforcements arrived, they surprise-attacked the British battery before moving into the cover of the fort. The orders were to spike the British cannons, then move back to the fort. The eager Americans were so successful they continued to chase the British and Indian forces into the woods where many Americans were killed. Some men inside the fort saw what was happening and screamed for their comrades to stop and come back. Today, some witnesses have spotted the ghost of an American soldier standing on the traverse and frantically waving his arms, trying to get the attention of someone on the other side of the river. "It would make sense that you might see somebody on top of the traverses waving their arms," Destatte said. "It ties into the written accounts."

There's still the mystery of the phantom woman and child in block-house number three. Though there's no written record of a woman and child taking cover in there, that's not the kind of event that would be recorded, either. John Destatte also notes that the sightings of the ghostly pair continue. After participating in an event at the fort one Sunday, Destatte returned to the office to drop off some things before going home when he met another volunteer who was getting ready to go home, too. He asked Destatte what the deal was with blockhouse number three. "I said, 'What are you talking about?'" Destatte said. "He told me there were a couple of girls here from southern Ohio, they'd never been here before, and they were just up on the traverse by blockhouse number three freaking out on Saturday night. I asked why and he said something about a woman and child and the block-house or something. I said, 'Oh, they're back again.' He said, 'What do you mean they're back again?' I told him the story and told him we hear the stuff occasionally."

Blockhouse number three is mainly used for storage today, and the tours don't go inside.

"You hear some stories too often to just totally disregard them," Destatte said.

# 9

# FORT ERIE

**War:** War of 1812 (1812–1814)
**Date of battle:** August 15, 1814
**Location:** Fort Erie, Ontario, Canada
**Participants:** 3,000 British troops under Lieutenant General Sir Gordon Drummond against 2,200 American troops under Brigadier General Edmund P. Gaines
**Casualties:** Over 3,500 men dead, wounded, missing, or captured

On the banks of the Niagara River just north of Buffalo, New York, a fort was built in 1764 as a response to the Seven Years War (1756–1763)—also known as the French and Indian War. The position is strategic—it sits near the mouth of a major river on Lake Erie and right at the edge of the waterline. The installation could protect ships and neighboring towns, and was the first line of defense on the Canadian border should the country's southern neighbor get rowdy, which of course it did during the American Revolutionary War. But it wasn't until the War of 1812—what many called the second American Revolution—that Fort Erie saw bullets fly. The fort changed hands many times during the two-year conflict; often the change of possession came without bloodshed because one side simply abandoned the fort. But there was one siege and battle that took place here where blood was spilt. This day stands out as among the bloodiest in Canadian history— a day that has led to many modern ghost encounters.

In 1803, Fort Erie was expanded up the hill away from the banks of the Niagara River offering a formidable vantage point and a more defendable position. On June 18, 1812, the United States declared war on England. At Fort Erie, the British hunkered in and kept their eyes on the river and lake before them, but no foreign force came. After a few months, the British determined that their soldiers were needed in battles elsewhere, so they dismantled what they could of the fort and pulled out. In 1813, American forces moved into Fort Erie for several months, but then pulled out in June. By December, the Brits moved back in for the winter and got to work cutting the fort in half so they could better defend it. This work continued through the following spring. On July 3, 1814, 3,500 American forces arrived on scores of boats from across the lake, and the show of force was so significant that all British options except surrender were eliminated.

The fort was in the charge of British Major Thomas Buck at the time, and 137 Redcoats were stationed inside when the Americans arrived. When Buck saw the many vessels carrying horses, field guns, and men, he knew the day would not belong to him. From farther south, 1,500 American men began a slow march toward Fort Erie, and no other British forces were in any position to offer Buck assistance. Major Buck ordered a few cannons fired at the Americans as a noble gesture to his own flag, but by the afternoon he was forced to throw the gates of the fort open and surrender.

The United States troops moved in and made the fort into a supply base. They also got to work expanding and reinforcing the fortress. The British built armaments to face the river and the lake to protect against a potential American invasion. When the Americans took over, their greater concern was an attack from inland, so the defenses needed to be repositioned.

Battles between the British and American forces were intensifying in the region. After the bloody battles of Chippewa and Lundy's Lane (which stands as Canada's bloodiest day), the Americans withdrew to Fort Erie, determined to keep a hold on southern Ontario. The stage was now set for a major standoff. The showdown came on August 13, 1814.

British Lieutenant General Sir Gordon Drummond ordered his 2,200 men to begin a siege. They let their cannon shells fly on the fort and the 3,000 Americans inside. The objective was to force the Americans to keep their heads down and distracted. The real action was going to begin in the pre-dawn hours of August 15.

On the 15th, while still under the cover of darkness, Drummond launched a most difficult military maneuver. Three columns of British soldiers were to attack separate targets on the fort from different directions. The first British column approached by wading through the lake—their task was to break the American line at Snake Hill on the right of the fort. As soon as the fighting began, the second column was supposed to begin their attack. But something went wrong for the British. The men sloshing through the water alerted the Americans who opened up their guns. The Redcoats broke ranks and the attack failed. The second column tried to begin their attack but by this time the entire fort was on high alert. The three British columns were now fighting en masse and tried three times to break through the American line, but were pushed back each time. Finally, on a fourth attempt, the British fought and clawed their way on to the northeastern bastion of the fort and were fighting the Americans inside. Seeing a break in the line, the other British soldiers pushed forward—an action that, though it made sense at the time, would prove disastrous. With hundreds of Redcoats lining the northeastern bastion, an ammunition chest in the fort ignited and the ensuing explosion killed hundreds of British men in a single blast. After the war had ended, the Americans claimed the fire was accidental. At the time, the British assumed other parts of the fort were booby-trapped with explosives as well and, those who could, retreated.

Many hundreds were dead or captured. Hundreds of others simply walked away from the battle and from the war. The British siege continued until September with both sides trading fire, and some of those shots found their marks with horrific accuracy. On September 5, under the cover of a heavy rainstorm, American Major General Jacob Brown launched an offensive attack against the British lines and broke through. The Americans overtook two British batteries, and they spiked the cannons and blew up the magazines. British Lieutenant-General Drummond quickly responded with a counterattack that drove the Americans back to the fort. In a letter dated September 21, 1814 to British Lt. Gen. Sir George Prevost, Drummond wrote: ". . . the sickness of the troops has increased to such an alarming degree, and their situation has really become one of such extreme wretchedness from the torrents of rain which have continued to fall for the last 13 days, and from the circumstances of the division being entirely destitute of camping equipage, that I feel it is my duty no longer to preserve in a vain attempt to maintain the blockade of so vastly superior and increasing a force of the enemy under the circumstances. I have therefore given orders for the troops to fall back to Chippewa . . ." On November 5, the Americans left Fort Erie for good, but not before they burned whatever was combustible and mined whatever could be exploded.

With such bloody engagements here, Fort Erie's haunted reputation is no surprise. To discuss the history and the ghosts more in-depth, I spoke with Jim Hill, the Superintendent of Heritage for the Niagara Parks Commission. He is responsible for all of the staffed heritage sites and about 120 plaques and markers along the Niagara River in Canada. Hill also had the opportunity to work at Fort Erie for ten years where he could explore the details of the battle, the ghosts, and some of the surprising archaeological evidence that actually supports parts of the fort's haunted reputation.

Hill first heard about the ghosts from the janitor at the fort—a gentleman who served 35 years in the Royal Canadian Air Force and worked at Fort Erie as his post-military occupation. Back in 1995, Hill played a role in starting up a Halloween program at the fort, and so he sought out the ghostly legends attached to the locale. "At Fort Erie there are mainly American ghosts, and a couple of them we think we know a fair bit about," Hill said. "Sergeant William Wait of the 11th U.S. infantry and Corporal Reed—that's who we think these guys were. And what we know of what happened to Sergeant Wait comes from Jarvis Hanks—a 14-year-old drummer in the 11th U.S. infantry."

According to Hill, not many people paid much attention to the accounts of Jarvis Hanks until a 1987 discovery.

"Before 1987, the most prominent ghostly legend attached to Fort Erie involves the ghosts of two American soldiers who wandered the banks of the Niagara River and the grounds near the old fort on a quest for something—we can only speculate as to what they were seeking. One soldier is headless, the other has no hands. Local folklore said that these figures needed each other because the headless figure couldn't see to help find whatever it was that they were looking for, and if they found what they were looking for, the hands-less figure couldn't pick it up."

So who was this 14-year-old eyewitness to the battle, and can his accounts be trusted? In *The Memoirs of Jarvis Hanks*, a work Hanks penned sometime between 1831 and 1847, he wrote of the incident he witnessed at Fort Erie:

*As there were no regular barbers attached to the army, the soldiers used to shave themselves, and each other. One morning several were shaving in succession, near a parapet. Sergeant Wait sat down facing the enemy, and Corporal Reed began to perform the operation of removing the beard from his face, when a cannon ball took the Corporal's right hand, and the Sergeant's head; throwing blood, brains, hair, fragments of flesh and bones, upon a tent near them, and upon the clothing of several spectators of the horrible scene. The razor also disappeared and no vestige of it was ever seen afterwards. The Corporal went to the hospital and had his arm amputated, and a few men rolled up the Sergeant's body in his blanket, carried it out and buried it. Probably less than 20 minutes transpired between the time he sat down to be shaved and the time he was reposing in the home of the soldier's grave.*

Not many scholars knew about *The Memoirs of Jarvis Hanks* before 1987, and certainly townspeople had little idea about this particular incident during the siege, a fact that lends much credence to the ghosts. But the question remains whether or not the event Jarvis Hanks wrote about actually happened.

"About a half a mile from the present British old Fort Erie, on the other end of the defense lines for the Americans, was a cornerstone for a massive fortified camp that the U.S. Army had," Hill said. "And at the far end there was a place they called Snake Hill or Towson's Battery. In that area there was a field hospital, and just beyond it was where they were burying the dead. In 1987, in one retired schoolteacher's backyard, they unearthed the remains of 28 American soldiers. One we're sure is Sergeant Wait."

Hill explained how this body was buried fully clothed. There is a little debate over the remains because the body wasn't buried with any clearly identifying marker such as a dogtag, but there is some evidence to suggest these may be Sgt. Wait's remains. "American sergeants wore epaulets," Hill said, "unlike British sergeants who wore chevrons or stripes. The epaulet had a different hook on it than the normal button that a soldier would have on his uniform. And there's absolutely no head, it's been disarticulated, and this guy has been buried fully clothed—you just weren't going to do that if a man received any medical attention because even then they knew they had to clean the guy up, clean his wounds, and get him out of his filthy uniform—they weren't complete barbarians when it came to this. And then four bodies down is a fellow who has been worked on, and he's buried in a shroud that was pinned up. This man had both of his arms amputated just above the elbow. We think that's the corporal who lingered for a day maybe, was worked on by the U.S. Army surgeons, and then didn't survive the wounding or the handiwork of the surgeons, which often could kill you. And he gets buried a couple spots down."

What makes this Fort Erie ghostly legend so intriguing is that first people talked about seeing two ghosts, one without hands, and one without a head. Then the memoir of an eyewitness is found, and then archaeologists find physical remains to back up the supernatural claims. Hill said that since the discovery of the remains in 1987, and the interment of the bodies with full military honors in Bath, New York, in 1988, the sightings of these two figures has ceased. But these two aren't the only ghosts said to be haunting Fort Erie.

Inside the museum at the Fort is a photograph taken a few years ago in what is called the British officer's kitchen in one of the large blockhouses at Fort Erie. "It's a fantastic photograph," Hill said. "The guy who took it is a professional photographer and he really did a nice job of capturing the way the room looks—the colors really jump out and the flames of the fire in the fireplace look great. Off to the left side of the picture, there is this white filmy shape that some people think looks like half a woman with her left shoulder and left hip and a skirt coming down."

The photo is a sought-after stop on tours, especially for school-children who are eager to hear about the ghosts. This curious photo of a misty female shape forces us to look back at the battle to see if there were any women there at the time.

Inside Fort Erie are two large blockhouses that the British built to house soldiers. The blockhouses were useful in peacetime, but considering their height, the upper levels weren't habitable during battle because they were easy targets for artillery. So only snipers and lookouts would have ventured to the upper levels. But the lower levels had some protection from the large earthworks that were dug around the fort and around important buildings.

The western blockhouse was used by the U.S. military as its mess house, or the place soldiers came to eat. "We know that American women were employed here," Hill said. "They were probably wives of soldiers, and they were employed as cooks and worked out of these structures—all of the rooms had fireplaces, so why not? We also know American women were paid as nurses, and we know women were living in these buildings when the British tried to storm the place and the far end of the western blockhouse got blown up.

"We know there were 19th U.S. infantry guys stuck in there at the time. They couldn't really get out partly because not only are there British and Canadians firing in one direction, but their own guys are firing in the other direction. The blockhouse has only one door, and if you'd stepped out to get out of that kitchen and onto the parade square, you'd have been mowed down by either side. So they're stuck in there when the place explodes."

Though there are no written records of any women dying in the blast, this is the location where some people have reported seeing a female apparition.

"We've heard these stories from folks who just wouldn't know the details that they were telling unless they read an awful lot of very detailed history about how people looked and who fought where," Hill said. "When you get an 8-year-old kid and a 19-year-old girl who really have no knowledge or interest in the stuff but in quite a bit of detail can tell you what they saw . . . I love those stories."

The final supernatural phenomenon that has been reported in and around Fort Erie involves streaks of bluish-green light.

Long before the War of 1812, the area that Fort Erie was built on was the land of the Algonquin and Iroquois Indians—two groups who didn't get along very well. There was a third group of Indians who lived along the Niagara River whose name has been lost to history. When the French arrived, they named this group the "Neutrals" because they traded with both the Algonquin and Iroquois. In an area on the Fort Erie property there is an Indian burial site that holds the remains of about 400 people. During 1950s and 1960s real estate development, these bones were uncovered and then shipped to Ottawa and various other locations where they could be placed on display. This obviously upset the local native community who lobbied to get the remains returned to their rightful place.

According to Jim Hill, in the early 1990s, the bones were all brought back to the land and reinterred in a large religious ceremony. The area is rife with aboriginal spirits.

The blue-green mists are said to be experienced most often in the winter because they stand in contrast to the white snow, and they've been seen streaking through Fort Erie, people's yards, and even occasionally into their homes. According to the local natives, this is a good omen and a sign of peace for the two great nations of the Niagara (the Algonquin and Iroquois Indians). They also say that to see fiery red streaks or spirits is a bad omen.

During Fort Erie's Halloween festivities and tours, their ghosts really come alive. The tour guides here share some of the many accounts staff and visitors have encountered over the years, and they use the ghosts to touch the real history that occurred on these grounds.

# Part VII

Texas Revolution

(1835–1836)

# 10

# THE ALAMO

**War:** Texas Revolution
**Dates of battle:** February 23–March 6, 1836
**Location:** San Antonio, Texas
**Participants:** General Antonio López de Santa Anna's Mexican army against William Barret Travis's Texas force of less than 200 troops inside the fort
**Casualties:** Roughly 800: 189 Texans and 600 Mexicans

*To the People of Texas & all Americans in the world—Fellow citizens & compatriots—I am besieged, by a thousand or more of the Mexicans under Santa Anna—I have sustained a continual Bombardment & cannonade for 24 hours & have not lost a man—The enemy has demanded a surrender at discretion, otherwise, the garrison are to be put to the sword, if the fort is taken—I have answered the demand with a cannon shot, & our flag still waves proudly from the walls—I shall never surrender or retreat . . . .*

—Lt. Col. William Barret Travis, in a letter dated February 24, 1836

The Alamo names are familiar, even legendary: Tennessee Congressman Davy Crockett, adventurer Jim Bowie, and future Mexican president Santa Anna. Over the years, the siege and battle that took place there in 1836 have been exploded to Texas-sized proportions. With the benefit of hindsight, we can see that military mistakes were made on both sides, but the end result cannot be disputed—hundreds were left dead in a very short period of time, and the war for Texas independence forged ahead. Though none of the Texas men who fought in the battle lived to recount the details, there were women, children, and Mexican soldiers whose accounts told the story. Today disembodied cries, apparitions from a bygone era, and other supernatural encounters tell us that the story is still being told.

*Photo by Valerie Prilop*

Originally called Misión San Antonio de Valero, the Alamo was built in 1724 as a Spanish mission and was used to convert the local Indians to Christianity. The converts were then used to farm the land that the missions now controlled. By 1793, the five San Antonio missions became secularized, and the land was distributed among the people who worked the land.

By the turn of the century, the Spanish military installed a cavalry unit into Misión San Antonio de Valero, and the soldiers stationed there referred to the building as "Alamo," the Spanish word for "cottonwood" in honor of the town the cavalry came from, Alamo de Parras, Coahuila. During Mexico's war for independence from Spain, the Alamo was occupied by Spanish/Royalist forces until it was taken over by Mexican Rebels who fought for their independence. The Mexicans held the Alamo until the Texas Revolution when the site became a serious point of contention.

October 2, 1835, marked the start of the Texas Revolution against Mexico to win its independence. Words between the two turned to actions, and actions beget bullets. The Mexican government had provided the residents of Gonzales—a town east of San Antonio—with a cannon to defend themselves against Indian raids. When tensions between Mexico and Texas escalated, the Mexican government sent about 100 men to get their cannon back. As the Mexican force approached, Texas Colonels John Moore and J. W. E. Wallace loaded the cannon with scraps of iron, took aim, and launched the first shot of the revolution. After a brief skirmish, the Mexicans retreated, and the revolution had begun. Armies were formed of volunteers, immigrants, and Tejano allies.

Over the next two months, other battles ensued—the Goliad Campaign, the Battle of Concepcion, and the Siege of Bexar (modern-day San Antonio). The Seige of Bexar, the first major battle of the conflict, was where the Mexican army surrendered the town (and the Alamo with it) to the Texans. Once the battle ended, many of the Texas military volunteers went home, figuring they accomplished their goal and it would be a matter of time before Mexico backed away.

In January of 1836, Colonel James Clinton Neill was in charge of the Alamo and its limited troops. If the fort was going to serve as Texas's first line of defense against Mexico, it would need more man-power. Neill sent letters to General Sam Houston pleading for more troops, horses, and supplies. Houston was caught by surprise by Neill's letter because the note implied that the Alamo was easy prey for their enemy. Major Green Jameson, the chief engineer who installed most of the firepower at the Alamo, bragged to Gen. Houston that the fort could "whip 10 to 1 with our artillery." Upon reading the news from Neill, Houston considered abandoning the fort altogether and pulling the troops stationed there back to a position they could truly fortify, but Governor Henry Smith didn't agree. Colonel James Bowie and a small group of volunteers left for San Antonio to help out.

Upon arrival, Col. Bowie was convinced that the Alamo was, indeed, the first and last line of defense between the Mexican army and the Anglo settlements. Bowie swore on his life that he would defend the fort. Governor Smith directed Lt. Col. William B. Travis and his cavalry to report to Neill. Only 30 horsemen responded to the order. On February 3, Travis and his men arrived, bringing the total force to roughly 150 men.

On February 14, Colonel Neill left the Alamo on furlough to tend to his family who had taken ill back in Bastrop. Col. Bowie and Lt. Col. Travis would share the responsibility of leading the fort. By February 23, a few issues became clear. Mexico didn't want to let the territory go so easily. Winning Bexar back was not only a matter of strategic importance, considering the town laid on one of the two main roads from the Mexican interior into Texas, it was also a point of pride to the Mexican military. On February 23, General Santa Anna came calling with over 1,000 troops. He intended to take the fort back.

Travis scribbled a hasty note: "The enemy in large force is in sight. We want men and provisions. Send them to us. We have 150 men and are determined to defend the garrison to the last." General Santa Anna sent word demanding surrender, and the Alamo responded with a single cannon blast. The siege of the Alamo had begun. For 24 hours, the Mexican forces bombarded the Alamo walls with cannon blasts.

In a letter he wrote, Travis's growing level of frustration was evident: "If my countrymen do not rally to my relief, I am determined to perish in the defense of this place, and my bones shall reproach my country for her neglect." He couldn't understand why his countrymen didn't heed his call for help. On March 1, 32 troops from Lt. George Kimbell's company broke through the Mexican line and made it into the Alamo. The men were a welcomed sight, but everyone inside knew it was not enough.

On the 12th day of the siege, Gen. Santa Anna announced a full-on assault would happen the following morning pre-dawn. Santa Anna's officers were perplexed. Their bombardments were taking down the outer walls, no significant show of Texas troops were any-where in the vicinity, and with a little more waiting, the men inside the Alamo would simply starve from lack of provisions and be forced to surrender. But Santa Anna wouldn't hear it. He insisted on storming in.

The next morning around 5 AM on Sunday, March 6, Santa Anna had his men concentrate their cannons and muskets on the Alamo from four directions. Over 1,000 Mexican troops marched on their target, and the Texans responded with cannon and musket shots of their own. The blow was enough to knock the Mexican forces back, but only for a brief period. They soon regrouped and overwhelmed the Alamo. Once inside, the hand-to-hand fight-ing was fierce. Some of the most accurate accounts of what happened within these now-hallowed walls come from the journals of the Mexican soldiers.

Lt. Col. José Enrique De la Peña wrote of Lt. Col. Travis's valor in battle:

*They had bolted and reinforced the doors, but in order to form trenches they had excavated some places that were now a hindrance to them. Not all of them took refuge, for some remained in the open, looking at us before firing, as if dumbfounded at our daring. Travis was seen to hesitate, but not about the death he would choose. He would take a few steps and stop, turning his proud face toward us to discharge his shots; he fought like a true soldier. Finally he died, but he died after having traded his life very dearly. None of his men died with greater heroism, and they all died. Travis behaved as a hero; one must do him justice, for with a handful of men without discipline, he resolved to face men used to war and much superior in numbers, without supplies, with scarce munitions, and against the will of his subordinates. He was a handsome blond, with a physique as robust as his spirit was strong.*

Travis's death wasn't the only demise De la Peña witnessed. There had been debate over whether Davy Crockett had died early in the battle or if he was one of the last men standing. According to De la Peña's testimony, Crockett was the last:

*Some seven men survived the general carnage and, under the protection of General Castrillón, they were brought before Santa Anna. Among them was one of great stature, well proportioned, with regular features, in whose face there was the imprint of adversity, but in whom one also noticed a degree of resignation and nobility that did him honor. He was the naturalist David Crockett, well known in North America for his unusual adventures, who had undertaken to explore the country and who, finding himself in Béjar at the very moment of surprise, had taken refuge in the Alamo, fearing that his status as a foreigner might not be respected. Santa Anna answered Castrillón's intervention in Crockett's behalf with a gesture of indignation and, addressing himself to the sappers, the troops closest to him, ordered his execution. The commanders and officers were outraged at this action and did not support the order, hoping that once the fury of the moment had blown over these men would be spared; but several officers who were around*

*the president and who, perhaps, had not been present during the*
*danger, became noteworthy by an infamous deed, surpassing the*
*soldiers in cruelty. They thrust themselves forward, in order to flatter*
*their commander, and with swords in hand, fell upon these unfor-*
*tunate, defenseless men just as a tiger leaps upon his prey. Though*
*tortured before they were killed, these unfortunates died without com-*
*plaining and without humiliating themselves before their torturers.*

When the battle was over, just three hours after it began, all 189 of the Texans who fought were now dead, and more than 600 Mexican soldiers lost their lives in the raid. The men of the Alamo fought bravely against overwhelming odds. Their fighting spirit and quiet pride have turned them into legends. "Remember the Alamo" has been uttered in other wars and campaigns ever since the Texas Revolution. The phrase doesn't refer to some battered stone church in San Antonio. It speaks of the 189 men who stood their ground for the land they believed in, even when so few of their countrymen came to their aid. It would take years for the Alamo legend to grow, but grow it did.

The haunted legends at the Alamo began within days of Gen. Santa Anna's victory.

J. R. Tipton has lived in the San Antonio area for more than 20 years. He runs the San Antonio Ghost Tours and recounted the early sighting. Santa Anna left the Alamo in the hands of Gen. Juan Jose Andrade and his men. "He still had about 1,500 men that were stationed here," Tipton said, "so Santa Anna got word back to them that he wanted the Alamo burned. So they sent some men over there to burn it down. As they got over to the Alamo, six 'Diablos' rose up out of the walls and they had balls of fire that turned into swords. They told the Mexican soldiers, 'You're not going to destroy the Alamo and to leave the church. The soldiers went back and it really upset the General, so he told them that he's going to take some men and he's going to go over there and when they're done burning it down, they're going to kill the cowards. They came back a little while later and all of the men loaded up and left town." The legend and even some of the written journals say that when Gen. Andrade returned to the Alamo, he also saw the six Diablos holding balls of fire.

Modern supernatural accounts are plentiful, and few know them better than Vincent Phillips, chief of the Alamo rangers and author of the forthcoming book, *The Alamo After Dark*. Phillips has worked as a ranger at the Alamo since 1999. The 50-year-old former Air Force officer got his start at the fort by working the evening and overnight security shifts when the park is closed (but not completely void of activity, according to many eyewitness accounts). "I started working the evening shift and then I went to the overnight shift," Phillips said. "I'd heard a few stories, but I really didn't learn that much about it until I started working the overnight shift."

Apparitions are the rarest-seen phenomena at the Alamo, but there are a few recognizable figures that pop up again and again, and not all of them are from the famous Alamo battle. According to Phillips, the specter of a Mexican soldier has appeared twice in recent years. "He is a soldier in a white uniform," Phillips said. "He has a canteen on his belt and a leather ammunition pouch hung from a strap over his shoulder. He carries a long gun, probably a British 'Brown Bess' musket, which was the most common firearm in Mexico's military inventory at the time.

"The white canvas uniform was meant to be worn in warm weather or as a utility uniform. Most of the Mexican troops in the Texas campaign wore the warmer and dressier blue wool uniform. Those in the Yucatan Battalion and possibly some of the other southern units had never been issued the blue uniform.

"The Mexican soldier was seen on the grounds at night by rangers. He was spotted at a distance the first time—he was there for a moment, and then he was gone. The second time he was in a different area of the complex. This encounter lasted longer and was much closer. An evening-shift ranger patrolling the grounds was walking past the cactus garden when, out of the corner of his eye, he saw a figure emerging from it. Slightly startled, the ranger stopped and turned toward it and then became really startled as the apparition came into focus.

"The soldier didn't appear to have an awareness of the ranger's presence. He made a right turn out of the cactus garden and walked quickly toward the acequia [the irrigation system that was constructed during the mission period]. He crossed over it at a spot where there is no bridge. He stepped through the air as if there were a solid walkway under his feet. After crossing the acequia, the ranger said the soldier suddenly went into an unnaturally fast pace—a kind of fast-forward, and disappeared around the southeast corner of the church."

After the Mexican soldier disappeared, the ranger got on his radio and called out to the other rangers on duty. They ran in the same direction that the soldier disappeared into, but they found no trace of anyone.

Another ghost from the battle Phillips described is that of an Alamo defender—a Texan who is seen in a white shirt, light brown pants, a long brown coat, and high black boots. This apparition appears outside of the Long Barracks with an excited and frantic look on his face, while fleeing the building with no weapon.

There are accounts of the battle that suggest some of the Texans were killed by their own men when they tried to surrender to the overwhelming Mexican force. The ghost Phillips describes is seen replaying like an old film reel. He sprints a few steps and then vanishes into the ether.

Some people try to label famous names such as Davy Crockett, Jim Bowie, and William Travis to the strange knocks, sounds, and other phenomena that occur inside, but there isn't much evidence to support the claim. What often happens at haunted locations is that any kind of supernatural event gets attributed to the most famous person who ever visited the location. Maybe we need to think that our ancestors, forefathers, or heroes from the past are still here and care about us. Maybe they do, and maybe it's a grave injustice to discount those who fought and died who didn't show up at the Alamo with a famous name and reputation.

It's not fair to assume the spectral Texan soldier seen running from the Long Barracks was one of the men who tried to surrender, but the circumstances do give us questions to ponder.

Chief Ranger Phillips has also had his share of unusual experiences while currently working at the Alamo. One of the most haunted hot spots is Alamo Hall, which is a former fire station. "I think there's one playful ghost who likes to get our attention by rattling doors and hardware, and knocking and banging," Phillips said. "Something that's very common, that we've pretty much all experienced, is if you're checking the French doors at night, you can pull on them as you're walking by to make sure they're secure. Then, after you walk away, it shakes again, like somebody else shook it just like you did. There's padlocks on certain doors and they'll swing. You stop it with your hand and walk away and it starts to swing again—things like that."

If the ghosts outside of Alamo Hall are playful, the forces inside seem to be considerably darker. "I don't know if it was a demon," Phillips said, "but it was definitely a malevolent presence in there. It would actually make contact with the rangers—physical contact. In one case, it even burned clothing. A ranger came out with a big burn mark on his shirt. He went in without it, he came out with it."

Could the burn marks hearken back to the legend of the six Diablos who wielded fire in front of the Mexican soldiers after the Alamo battle? The legend is so fantastic that it's easy to discount, but the Diablos were reported by two separate groups of Mexican Army officers. To have a ranger's shirt burned by some unseen force begs the question of the Diablos, at the very least.

"Alamo Hall is the creepiest building I've personally ever been in," Phillips said. "You can just feel it all over you when you go in there at night. If it's full of people, you wouldn't feel it so much, but when you go in there and it's just one or two of you, you do. It was getting worse and worse in there until people didn't even want to go in there and check it anymore to see if it was secure."

Other apparition sightings on these grounds include the ghost of a cowboy who would have been from the late 1800s when cowboys used to bring their cattle right into Alamo Square to buy and sell them. Who the phantom cowboy is, how he died, and why he is still around is a mystery. A ghostly woman has also been seen inside. Some visitors will point past a locked gate and ask who that woman is sitting on the bench only to watch her disappear. She may be one of the women who took refuge inside the fort during the siege, or maybe she's another who is simply passing by. Considering that this fort was a military base for the Spanish, Mexicans, Texans, and United States and even the Confederate armies at one point, there is a significant amount of history and ghostly sightings that won't let us forget the Alamo.

# *Part VIII*

Post-War of 1812

(CIRCA 1840)

# 11

# FORT GEORGE

**War:** Post-war of 1812
**Location:** Niagara-on-the-Lake, Ontario, Canada
**Participants:** British

Life on a military base has never been easy. Quarters can be cramped for the soldiers and their families, privacy scarce, food and supplies are often not of the highest quality (to put it kindly), and many times soldiers have to relocate, sometimes dragging their immediate families far from home (and sometimes leaving their spouses and children behind altogether). We know there is a cost to war—we need only to turn on the television or read a newspaper to learn about soldiers dying. But there is a cost of war that is often overlooked, a cost that 150 years ago was even ignored—the hardships and casualties the families of soldiers face during life on the base. The harsh conditions can lead to sickness, disease, and even death. Fort George has its share of ghosts related to the heavy fighting that took place here during the War of 1812, but there is one little spirit that demands some attention for those non-soldiers who sometimes gave their lives for someone else's cause.

The 1783 Treaty of Paris gave Fort Niagara on the shores of Lake Ontario in western New York to the Americans. The British response was Fort George—a base that would serve as the British military headquarters in Canada located across the lake on the Canadian side and visible from Fort Niagara. Fort George was completed in 1802 and was the site of a fierce battle from May 25–27, 1813, during the War of 1812. The American army captured Fort George and used the site as an invasion point into upper Canada over the coming months. By December, the British were able to take Fort George back and hold it throughout the duration of the war and for many years after. It was during this peacetime period several decades after the last shots of the War of 1812 had been fired that we find a most intriguing ghost encounter.

This story came up during my conversation with Jim Hill, the Superintendent of Heritage for the Niagara Parks Commission. It was during the first summer that Fort George began offering ghost tours that Hill heard about this peculiar new ghost. "I was just a security guy there at the time, and my friend Kyle [Upton] was the guy who convinced Parks Canada to let them have this ghost tour," Hill said. "We were well into the summer that year, and we started taking people back to the Angel Inn (a pub in Niagara-on-the-Lake) for a pint and to tell us their ghost stories."

At the Olde Angel Inn, Hill and his friend Kyle noticed that two couples waited until all the others in the crowd of about 16 thinned out. Hill said, "This one lady said she's embarrassed to say this, but she has certain feelings or sometimes sees things. She said, 'I saw something on the tour.' And we said, 'Oh yeah?' And then I saw the look on her husband's face was not embarrassment or even pride, it was sort of concern for his wife— that he was worried about her. Like maybe she shouldn't talk about it or think about it. So that added to the eeriness of it. During the tour, we took people into these blockhouses that have big, heavy internal stairwells that takes you up to the second level of the blockhouse. It's an open stairwell and you can see it from all sides. Halfway through, Kyle was talking about a ghost that we call Irving who was, what we think, kind of a poltergeist character that would do little tricks and tug on the bottom of people's coats and stuff like that to get their attention. In the 1960s, somebody randomly named this figure Irving and that kind of stuck. I remember when I started working there in the mid-1980s: Irving is the ghost in the blockhouse.

"The woman said that while Kyle was talking, this little figure came down the stairs in what she thought at first was a dress, but she realized that on looking at it a little more closely it looked like a man's shirt. She said the child had extremely short hair and sat and listened to the story, and then followed the group out. When you get to the middle of Fort George there is this lovely, yellow officer's quarters, and when we got to that point the little figure stopped in the path, and this lady said that as the group moved away, she kept looking back and this little figure didn't follow. She said, 'I can tell you that this little person's name is Sarah Ann. Once I saw short hair, I thought it was a little boy. But no, her name is Sarah Ann.'"

Sarah Ann—it certainly takes a bit of audacity to go on a ghost tour and imply they've given their ghost the wrong name and gender. But Jim Hill and Kyle Upton were certainly intrigued with the level of detail that they heard. Intrigued enough to do a little digging.

"There is this 220-year-old Anglican church in town, and they kept pretty good records for the town and for the garrison as well," Hill said. "They tracked people getting sick, people being born, and people dying. So we talked to the rector there and we also talked for a while about this to one of the senior history guys at Parks Canada who had been at Fort George, and what we found was interesting right off the bat. Why did the girl have a man's shirt on instead of a dress? And why did she have short hair? It turns out that to fight lice, the lower classes often kept young kids' hair shorn pretty tight. And why did she stop at the officer's quarters? We know that even before the U.S. Army captured the place in 1813, the British were in the process of cutting it in half. They thought it was too big to defend, so they did this to a lot of their forts. They had a few Canadian militiamen, a few Indians, and very few regular army Redcoats, so how do you defend these big stupid things you built? You cut them in half. They leveled the officer's quarters, cut Fort George literally almost right down the middle, and eventually put a gun battery there. When the U.S. Army captured it they expanded on that and thought it was a good idea, too [*laughs*] and built up the defenses even more.

"We also wanted to find if there were any records from the war of 1812 period concerning a young girl. There are some pretty good records that survived, but we didn't find anything, though this lady had creeped us out pretty bad. There was an old gentleman that worked at St. Mark's as a groundskeeper in this old cemetery who said to us, 'There's a Sarah Ann buried here and she was a British soldier's daughter.' Holy cow, no kidding? We go over and there is this tombstone. It names her father, and his regiment; he's a troop Sergeant Major with the Queens Dragoon guards. Sarah Ann had died at age 7 in 1840. We said this is totally wrong. Fort George was bashed to pieces at the end of the War of 1812. They built another fort on the other side of Niagara-on-the-Lake called Fort Mississauga where they housed all the troops well out of cannon range of the U.S. Army. And that was an active base right up until the 1960s."

Hill and Upton did some more digging and learned some more facts related to the area surrounding Fort George. In the mid-1830s, the British poured troops into Canada to help stop the Republican uprising—a group of Canadians who wanted independence from British rule. In 1837 and 1838, the Upper Canada Rebellion and Lower Canada Rebellion took up arms against the Redcoats. Both uprisings were crushed and their leaders vilified. So, by 1840, there were still a large number of British forces stationed in Canada to help keep the peace. "In particular the British poured in cavalry—almost what amounted to a constabulary," Hill said. "This regiment or squadron of Dragoon guards was posted to Niagara, and the infantry guys, the local Canadian infantry militia, were housed in tents well away from the river at Butler's Barracks. But of course the cavalry have horses, so where do you corral the horses on this huge common? Well you've got old Fort George with deep ditches, and with some of the picketing still there so you have a nice fenced-in corral, basically. So the only fellows staying in what was left of Fort George were these Dragoons."

Today Fort George looks the way it would have when it was first constructed. There are a few original buildings, but most of the earthworks and other structures were recreated. We have to remember that the British cut the fort in half so they could defend it more easily. So for the spirit of the little girl, she stopped where the old Fort George would have ended back in 1840. "This woman nailed the appearance of a child of a common soldier pretty well for the 19th century," Hill said. "She had the location right, why the kid stopped where she did stop, and I mean nobody, not even people who worked at Fort George for many years, knows about it being cut in half. Because you don't want to start your tour saying during the war it looked nothing like this—it changed its appearance a couple of times based on where the British wanted defenses and where the U.S. Army engineers wanted them.

"So this woman nailed the appearance, and she knew nothing about the history of the area and nothing about the history of the British army, knew nothing about these little minor Republican rebellions that even Canadian kids don't get taught about, and even we didn't know about how Dragoons were stationed here and actually used the place during the rebellion period. There were a lot of facts that suddenly came out that I didn't know all because of this lady who named the kid and had the age about right."

There are no monuments or plaques built in recognition of the families that get uprooted and sometimes torn apart by military life. The wives, husbands, and children of soldiers also make the ultimate sacrifice at times, and maybe it's important that one or two of their ghosts stick around to remind us of the total cost of war.

# Part IX

United States Civil War

(1861–1865)

# 12

# VALVERDE BATTLEFIELD

**War:** United States Civil War (1861–1865)
**Dates of battle:** February 20–21, 1862
**Location:** Socorro County, New Mexico
**Participants:** 3,000-man Union Army under
Colonel Edward R. S. Canby against 2,500 Confederates under
Brigadier General Henry H. Sibley and Colonel Thomas Green
**Casualties:** 389

The Confederate States of America had a plan: to establish themselves as the ruling government from the Atlantic to the Pacific Ocean. By pushing Union forces out of New Mexico, Arizona, and California, the Confederate government would span the entire American landmass— a move that would significantly help increase their legitimacy with foreign countries, especially potential foreign trading partners. The Union also knew the perceptual importance of the Southwest, and they weren't going to let it go without a fight. Valverde in New Mexico is the site of one clash between the Union and Confederate armies. Today the site is a ghost hunter's dream, not only because of how supernaturally active the land is, but due to the site's remote location, it's also free of human contamination.

The Union Army had established itself at Fort Craig, located 125 miles north of Las Cruces. The fort was built in 1854 as a base of U.S. operations against the Indians of the region. When the Civil War began, it became a Union stronghold. Colonel Edward R. S. Canby had 1,200 troops under his command at the fort in 1862. When Col. "Kit" Carson and his 1st New Mexico Cavalry arrived, the numbers approached 4,000 Union men. The fort was so full that some soldiers were forced to pitch tents outside the security of the walls.

On the Confederate side, Brigadier General Henry H. Sibley and 2,500 of his men were on the march from their temporary headquarters in El Paso. The Confederates had hoped to engage Col. Canby on the open plain just a mile south of the fort, but Canby didn't bite, so Sibley forged a new plan. The Confederates withdrew 7 miles down the river and crossed in a shallow area. The new objective was to march up the opposite bank of the Rio Grande, get north of Fort Craig, cross back over at the ford at Valverde, and cut the supply and communications line between the Union fort and their headquarters in Santa Fe.

When Col. Canby saw the Confederates march up the opposite bank of the Rio Grande, he ordered more than 3,000 of the Union soldiers at the base to the ready. Canby knew Valverde was where the Confederates would try and cross, and he commanded his men to get there first.

The Union force reached the ford in the Rio Grande, crossed over, and engaged the Confederates in the shadow of Black Mesa. The battle had begun on the evening of February 20, 1862.

Col. Canby attacked first but was quickly repelled by Confederate cannon and small arms fire. The Union pulled back and engineered a military first—a guided bomb. They strapped a mule with explosives and tried to direct the animal toward the Confederate line. The results were deadly, though only for the mule.

At dawn the next morning the fighting began anew with more vigor than the evening before. Union artillery had arrived and proved effective at keeping the Confederates away from the river. The Union was working to come around the right flank of the Confederates while Union Captain Alexander McRae pounded their left flank, forcing the Rebels to spread out and thin their lines. By noon, the Federal forces were showing the upper hand.

Just after 3 PM, Col. Canby made the decision to advance his right and center units to concentrate fire on the Confederate left flank. The Confederates pushed back but were repelled by Capt. McRae's artillery fire. A Texan lancer division of the Confederate army charged a second time and managed to overrun the Union guns. Savage hand-to-hand combat ensued and Capt. McRae's men suffered a thrashing. The Union line fell apart as some men dropped their weapons and ran back toward the river. Eighty percent of the Union losses during the battle happened at this point and in the span of only minutes. One soldier under McRae, upon seeing his comrades overpowered, fired his musket into the gunpowder kegs—a suicidal act that ensured the Confederates would never make use of the precious wartime commodity.

At battle's end, 222 Union men were killed or wounded compared to 183 Confederate. Victory was claimed by the Rebel side; however, Union forces never lost control of Fort Craig. After the Civil War ended, Fort Craig and the Valverde Battlefield were left for the New Mexico plains to swallow up again. No development of any kind has ever come to Valverde, making the site a ghost hunter's dream.

Cody Polston is the founder and president of the Southwest Ghost Hunters Association (SGHA). He and his group have visited the Valverde site on several occasions. Polston told me that the land where the battle was fought is private property owned by media mogul Ted Turner. Polston and his group received permission to conduct a ghost investigation there.

I asked him how he first heard Valverde may be haunted. "The first story I heard was when I was at a local bar," Polston said. "We have T-shirts for SGHA that have our logo on the front, and on the back it says, 'I'm a ghost hunter. If you see me running, try to keep up.' Someone in the bar saw that and said, 'Yeah, so-and-so saw something down at the battlefield,' and he pointed me toward this big, redneck-looking cowboy guy. So I started talking to him, and he was very leery to talk about it until a couple beers later."

"What did he say he saw?" I asked.

"He said he was riding near there and was looking for a lost calf," Polston said. "He crossed over the river, and he was on the other side of the Mesa and was searching down there. He said it was getting close to dark and the sun was just starting to go down when he saw a headless Confederate soldier pop up out of the bushes and shoot a musket at him. He got the hell out of there and he refuses to go out on the ranch at night now—at least on that part. You could tell, because of his reluctance to talk about it, because he wouldn't talk about it when anyone else was around, and a big guy like that isn't going to admit to being scared of anything, that this guy meant it.

"So, from that story and the fact that we knew there were things going on at Fort Craig from speaking with the Bureau of Land Management, we thought 'Why not the battlefield?'"

In addition to the story from the ranch hand at the bar, Cody Polston was also e-mailed an account from someone who said he worked on the freight train that runs near the battlefield. While heading north, this gentleman claimed he witnessed a full-on charge of what he thought was a reenactment group practicing, considering there was no audience. He didn't find out until later that reenactments are never performed at Valverde, and considering that ranch hands patrol the area, what this man saw could not have been anyone living.

There was enough evidence for the SGHA to proceed with an investigation.

So many battlefields are preserved as historic parks because they are hallowed ground where men and women took their last breaths for their cause. While preservation of historic sites is important work, in the realm of ghost hunting, a preserved site can make for a contaminated investigation scene. For example, at the Gettysburg, Pennsylvania, battle site, there are Civil War reenactors walking around the town and the battlefield almost every day of the year. There are tourists at Gettysburg clicking photos during all hours that the park is open. There's so much living human activity at Gettysburg that conducting a paranormal investigation is difficult considering the many false positives that recording devices and environment-reading equipment will pick up. But Valverde offers a unique opportunity—there are no roads, houses, or streetlights anywhere around. Without permission to go on the property and a map, you'll never know where to find the actual battle location. Valverde was virgin territory for Cody Polston and the SGHA.

When conducting an investigation, Polston first sends in a reconnaissance team as phase one of a three-phase process. On his first visit to the site he brought four others from his team with him. "The recon phase goes out and gets the stories, they videotape, they get the maps and all that, and when the ghost hunters go in, they kind of go in blind," Polston said. "They know on the map what's happened where, but they don't know what the incident is. The logic here is to prevent investigator bias.

"We knew the area around McRae's cannons was one of the hot spots—it's where a lot of people reported seeing things, and it's where the ranch hand saw the Confederate guy shoot at him. So we focused around the area of the cannons."

"What kind of equipment was brought on the initial investigation?" I asked.

"The main instrument we were using was a natural tri-field meter," Polston said. The tri-field meter is a device that measures electromagnetic fluctuations in a small area surrounding the meter. This device takes its measurements from three axis points to determine the readings. "For curiosity's sake, we took a couple of AC field meters [a device that measures alternating electromagnetic current] based on a hypothesis, but we didn't get anything on those. But the natural tri-field were going off. Of course you always have to look at your data, so we went back and thought maybe there was a large pocket of water or something amplifying the magnetic field, maybe what's going on was something geophysical, or some space storms. We're checking out all the sources and there was just nothing."

SGHA went out for a second investigation, though that excursion yielded nothing worth noting, but the third time they went was February 26, 2005, near the anniversary of the battle. They hiked a mile into the site and began recording with handheld video cameras with infrared capabilities—these are basically video cameras with a night vision capability that looks further into the infrared part of the spectrum where the unaided human eye can't see. Paranormal investigators sometimes pick up anomalies with these types of cameras. Cody Polston and the SGHA also brought along their tri-field meters and some audio recording equipment to try and record Electronic Voice Phenomena (EVP). EVP has been around almost as long as portable recording equipment but rose to prominence in the early 1980s and has experienced a significant surge in use in the last few years, as many ghost hunters have incorporated the concept of trying to capture spirit voices as part of their standard investigation practice. Travel to the Valeverde battle site was hard going for Polston and his group. They couldn't bring many of their preferred observation tools such as digital video recorders and other cumbersome surveillance equipment. But they could bring handheld video cameras with some infrared capability and their portable audio recorders. The audio evidence they captured was incredible.

At the site where Captain McRae and his men were overrun in such a short period of time on February 21, 1862, one of the SGHA investigators turned on her audio recorder and asked the question, "Who is your commanding officer?" After a two- or three-second pause, a male voice very slowly and clearly says, "Captain McRae."

"It's important to ask questions that are relevant and that there's no mistaking what it's [the EVP] saying," Polston said. "And that was recorded right where the charge happened back then—it kind of freaked us out."

Polston said his group captured many other strange recordings during that investigation, mainly pops and clicks that one may interpret as distant gunfire, but he said he can't rule out that they're something perfectly natural like someone nearby stepping on a dry stick or twig.

Polston and his team captured other evidence as well. In addition to the EVP, he captured several photographs at Valverde that offer up something to ponder. Polston's wife is an optics technician and helped him modify his digital camera to capture more of the infrared part of the electromagnetic spectrum.

The concept of spirit photography—or capturing some kind of potentially supernatural photo anomaly—hinges on one big question: Can the camera see more than the human eye? The answer is yes. Both film and digital cameras can discern the environment faster than the human eye because they can freeze time. Typical shutter speeds for cameras are 1/250th of a second. Cameras can, of course, be set to slower and much faster shutter speeds, but 1/250th of a second is pretty average for everything from disposable cameras to your basic digital camera—the reason being that at slower speeds your pictures are likely to come out blurry if you don't have a steady hand or overexposed if the conditions are too bright.

Both film and digital cameras don't discriminate in regard to the subject of the photo, meaning when you look at any object: the page of this book, for example, you are focused on these words and this page. There are things going on off the page too, of course. There may be a hand holding the book up, a desk underneath it, maybe a lamp beside it, and a myriad of other objects that are in our homes, offices, and the world around us. But your mind is intentionally tuning out these other objects because you're focusing right here. If there was a camera where your eye is right now that just clicked a picture, you would be able to see the book, the hand, and any other objects around the book in the field of view. Because this is a frozen piece of time, you could take your time to study the image for objects and possible anomalies you may have missed because your attention was focused for the purpose of reading.

Digital cameras bring another element to the anomaly discussion— they can and do see beyond the visible light spectrum into ultraviolet and infrared depending on the software configuration of the charge coupled device (CCD) or the brain of the camera. Digital cameras are not intelligent. When the camera user presses the button, the shutter opens and electromagnetic energy filters in through the lenses. If the camera determines there is something prominent at the very edge of the visible light spectrum, or the portion of the electromagnetic spectrum that we can see, then it captures this information on the image.

Polston altered the infrared lens filter on his digital camera in order to see a little further into that part of the spectrum, where ghosts and spirits may just dwell. Here are the results from some daytime photos taken at the Valverde battlefield:

*Photos by Cody Polston*

You'll notice by the prominent tree in the background that this photo was taken in the same spot, and Polston said they were taken just a few seconds apart from each other. They were shocked to see the very obvious shadowy figure in both images. "These photos caused us to ask more questions," he said. "Is it an apparition or is it energy? If it's energy, then what's it doing there? What's causing it?"

I asked Cody what his group determined the shadows to be. He said, "I have skeptics in my group that watched too much *Scooby Doo* as a child. They think everything is explainable, but it's the whole element of the mystery that they're drawn to. One of the things they said was maybe this was something on the lens, but it shifted positions so it really can't be something on the lens. Then they suggested something called CCD residual, which happens when it's dark; you photograph something bright, you take another picture and that part of the picture might make its way into the next image. But these pictures were taken in the daytime, so you can rule that out. These pictures kind of stumped the skeptics as well."

The SGHA said they're planning future investigations at the Valverde battlefields, and they're also hoping to play a role in working with the Bureau of Land Management to help get the site preserved as an historic location that others may visit in the future. Like many paranormal investigators, history is as sacred to Cody Polston and the SGHA as the ghosts are.

Valverde offers paranormal investigative groups such as SGHA the opportunity to study ghosts in a preserved location. Though the land may have reclaimed any evidence of the battle fought here long ago, history and the ghosts who still wander the grounds have not forgotten who died here and why.

# 13

# ANTIETAM

**War:** United States Civil War (1861–1865)
**Date of battle:** September 17, 1862
**Location:** Sharpsburg, Maryland
**Participants:** 87,000-man Union Army under
General George B. McClellan against 40,000-man
Confederate Army under General Robert E. Lee
**Casualties:** 23,110

*On the forenoon of the 15th, the blue uniforms of the Federals
appeared among the trees that crowned the heights on the eastern
bank of the Antietam. The number increased, and larger and
larger grew the field of the blue until it seemed to stretch as far
as the eye could see, and from the tops of the mountains down
to the edges of the stream gathered the great army of McClellan.*
—Lt. Gen. James Longstreet,
Army of Northern Virginia

September 17, 1862, was the bloodiest day of the American Civil War.
The air burned with smoke and fire from the musket balls, cannons, and
other ordinance that flew from General George McClellan's Union army
toward General Robert E. Lee's Confederates who answered in kind.
Those who were there and fought in the bloody battle, like Lt. Col. A. S.
"Sandie" Pendleton of the Confederate army, assumed this day would be

their last. "Such a storm of balls I never conceived it possible for men to live through. Shot and shell shrieking and crashing, canister and bullets whistling and hissing most fiend-like through the air until you could almost see them. In that mile's ride I never expected to come back alive," Pendleton wrote of the ordeal. With so much blood spilled in so little time, it's not surprising that the Antietam battlefield is one of America's most haunted battle sites.

During August 1862, General Lee and his Confederate Army were coming off a huge victory in Manassas, Virginia. Lee headed to northern Virginia and Maryland, hoping to pick up more men and supplies. Union Gen. McClellan and his army followed Lee to the town of Frederick where Gen. McClellan came into the rather lucky possession of the Confederate battle plan, Lee's Special Order No. 191. Special Order No. 191 outlined Lee's plan for an invasion of Maryland and detailed Confederate troop movements. By bringing the fight into northern territory, Lee knew the Federal troops would be forced to drop back and defend Maryland and Washington—which meant pulling out of war-battered Virginia. Upon reading the document, Union Gen. McClellan said, "Here is a paper with which, if I cannot whip Bobby Lee, I will be willing to go home."

McClellan pressed west in the first two weeks of September while Gen. Lee split his army, sending troops under Gen. Thomas "Stonewall" Jackson to Harpers Ferry for its capture. But McClellan didn't split his forces—he kept his eyes on Lee. On September 14, in the passes of South Mountain, the Union and Confederate armies collided. Significantly outnumbered, Gen. Lee hoped to delay the Federal forces so he could regroup his entire army. The Union pressed through, and by the next afternoon both armies had set their front lines on the east and west sides of Antietam Creek near Sharpsburg, Maryland. On the 16th, Gen. Jackson's forces caught up with Lee and over 120,000 men suspected a major battle was in the works. By dawn the next morning, those suspicions were confirmed.

Union Gen. Joseph Hooker's artillery fired the first shots—a thunderous volley of fire and ordinance aimed at Gen. Jackson's men who were ducked in the cornfields north of town. Hooker later described the cornfield as looking as though it had been cut down with a knife and laid neatly in a row like fallen soldiers. For almost an hour, Gen. Jackson's men sat exposed and could only hope that the awesome firepower didn't cut them down like the cornstalks. The Federals charged before the Confederate line was reinforced and the Union men were driven back.

*I was lying on my back, supported on my elbows, watching the shells explode overhead and speculating as to how long I could hold up my finger before it would be shot off, for the very air seemed full of bullets, when the order to get up was given, I turned over quickly to look at Col. Kimball, who had given the order, thinking he had become suddenly insane.*

—Lt. Matthew J. Graham, Company H, 9th New York Volunteers

*Each discharge was at first discernable, but after a little grew so rapid from all the guns brought into play from both sides that it became one prolonged roar.*

—Col. Adoniram Judson Warner, 10th Pennsylvania Reserves

In other parts of the battlefield, the taking and giving of ground was similar. Union forces under Gen. French collided with Confederates under Generals Hill and Longstreet and fought for almost four hours along a sunken road near Roulette and Piper farms. Neither side overtook the other, and both withdrew out of exhaustion, but not before so many were left dead on a road that would earn the new moniker "Bloody Lane."

*A photo taken at Sunken Road shortly after the battle. Photo courtesy of the Library of Congress*

In the southeastern part of town, Federal Gen. Burnside and his men tried to cross a bridge over Antietam Creek for more than three hours but were driven back each time by 400 Confederate men from Georgia who yielded only after costing the Union troops a toll of many lives. In the afternoon, Gen. Hill, who was initially left behind at Harpers Ferry, arrived and joined in the battle, driving Union Gen. Burnside's men back to the bridge they had captured earlier that afternoon. In the late afternoon, the last shots of the battle of Antietam echoed on the ears of those who could still hear after a day of explosions, which battered the eardrums of everyone in gun range.

In no other American war to date have more soldiers died in the course of one day than at Antietam. When the sun set, the Union suffered 12,410 losses and the Confederates lost 10,700. In the space of only 12 square miles, more than 23,000 were dead. In every direction one looked, there were bodies. Though neither side could claim a decisive victory, the battle changed the war because it was clear to the Union Generals that this wasn't some minor rebellion they were dealing with. This war wasn't going to be over anytime soon.

Though there was no real victor of the battle, Antietam had many other implications—all of which favored the Union. The next morning, Gen. Lee and his Confederate troops crossed the Potomac River and headed south, temporarily abandoning their plans for a northern invasion. Upon hearing of the loss, the British government postponed their plans of legally recognizing the Confederate States of America; and within days, President Abraham Lincoln was moved to sit down and draft the Emancipation Proclamation, which would free all of the slaves in the southern states. Lincoln made this move in an effort to crush the southern economy, thus weakening the Confederate military, and to make the war not just about preserving the union, but a moral war where the righteous fought to free enslaved men. It is worth noting that the Emancipation Proclamation did not free slaves in Union states such as Maryland and Missouri—Lincoln didn't want these states who were on the edge moving their support over to the Confederacy.

Antietam was a prelude of what was to come in the American Civil War—more bloody days, battles, and years lay ahead. From the personal accounts of those who fought near Sharpsburg, we can see the fear and wide-eyed shock that each participant must have had at seeing the seas of enemy soldiers firing muskets by the hundreds while cannons and explosives launched and rained down from every direction. So many men must have assumed that this would be their final day, and of course for many thousands on both sides, it was. This incredible sense of fear, rage, and doom left an impression on Antietam that has led the location to be counted among the most haunted.

Patrick Burke is a paranormal investigator, president of the American Battlefield Ghost Hunters Society, and is the author of the book, *Battlefield Guide to Ghost Hunting*. The 48-year-old has been interested in military history and the paranormal since his childhood. He also served in the United States Air Force, where he picked up some reconnaissance techniques that he brings to his ghost investigations. Burke says he's a sensitive who can often sense, hear, and see ghosts. During an early-October investigation at Antietam, Burke and some of the newer members of his group were walking through the Sunken Road area of the battlefield near the Irish Monument. "We were at Sunken Road, and out of the corner my eye, I see some movement. You know how a lot of people, once they see movement, they want to turn their head and see what it is. But if you stay steady and still long enough, the environment will wrap around you—you become part of the environment. If I see something out of the corner of my eye, I just use my peripheral vision—it's good enough that it will pick up details. At Sunken Road I saw this sort of white form running past the right side of the Irish monument."

"Did you get a sense as to who it might have been?" I asked.

"I assumed he was an Irishman," Burke said. "That's probably just intuition, but from a historical point of view, I know that the Confederates didn't go to that side. That's where the Irish Brigade came, infiltrated the right flank, and shot right down the lane and wiped out the Confederates."

This wasn't Burke's only paranormal experience during this Antietam visit. After seeing the Irish soldier dash by, Burke went alone into Sunken Road and hunkered down for about 20 minutes. "I started hearing men moving," he said. "I started hearing the accoutrements of their equipment, and I heard one person say, 'Now? . . . Now?' 'No yet . . . not yet.'"

I asked Burke what he felt offered the best chances for those who wanted to experience the paranormal at a battlefield for themselves. Was there a particular battlefield? A particular time of day or time of year?

"Is the person going there with an open mind or are they actually going there to have a paranormal experience?" Burke asked. "There's some people in the scientific community that say if you're looking for it, it's going to happen and that disqualifies it. My intuitive science method says that you go to the site more than once, and you go there with an open mind. I go to these sites and say, 'What happened? Share with me.' I'm not necessarily expecting something to happen, but you can anticipate that something may happen. If you go to these places with an open mind, then you can have the paranormal experience at any battlefield and at any time."

Most of Burke's experiences have been in the evenings when he and his group have conducted overnight investigations and campouts. But nighttime isn't mandatory. Plenty of people have witnessed the supernatural during daylight as well.

Ron Hughes is an independent paranormal researcher based in Maryland whom I've known for many years. He's been to Antietam a number of times as both a tourist and an investigator. I asked him what he felt was the most active part of the battlefield. "Everyone says Bloody Lane, but that's not the case," Hughes said. "It's the area between the cornfield and the Mumma Cemetery, which sits directly behind the Visitor Center— that's where a lot of the fighting took place. These guys sat 50 yards apart and just cut each other down through the corn. That area is very active. I got an EVP [Electronic Voice Phenomena] in the Mumma Cemetery. I set the recorder to voice activate and left it on the wall back in the far-left corner, which would probably be about 55 to 60 yards back to my left.

"A bird activated the recorder, and then after that it sounds like the din of battle—a whole lot of mayhem, a whole lot of noise, like a lot of yelling. And then above all this you hear a voice yell, 'Load muskets. Go!' Load muskets. Go. It's really clear. Like a command."

The Mumma's family cemetery pre-dates the Civil War and was also the site of some of the fighting, which may explain Hughes's fascinating EVP capture. This audio evidence of something beyond our normal understanding is what drives people like Hughes to continue to study these phenomena at sites such as Antietam.

## General James "Ole Pete" Longstreet, Confederate States of America

Born January 8, 1821, died January 2, 1904

General James Longstreet was one of the most notable leaders of the American Civil War. He earned the respect of both his colleagues and enemies by being a masterful offensive tactician. Though Longstreet's battle style often contrasted with General Lee's more aggressive and straight-ahead approach, Lee still referred to Longstreet affectionately as his "Old War Horse." But Longstreet's friends and family called him "Pete."

*Photo courtesy of the Library of Congress*

In the days and hours leading up to the battle of Antietam, Generals Longstreet and Hill found themselves on the Piper Farm property. Henry and Elizabeth Piper's farm included an apple orchard, cornfields, and other crop fields that were freshly plowed to receive the winter wheat planting. The Pipers, who were reportedly Unionists, also owned slaves who lived in a stone building beside the well. The entire property lay right in the middle of General Lee's battle plans, and Confederate Generals Hill and Longstreet arrived to commandeer the house to use as their headquarters.

The evening of their arrival, the Pipers' daughter, Mary Ellen, served the generals dinner and then offered them some wine out of courtesy. Longstreet initially refused, but then thought better of it when Hill partook. Longstreet said to his hostess, "I will thank you for some of that wine."

After dinner, the Generals asked the Piper family to leave because the battle was inevitable and their home would not be safe. The family left everything they had in the care of Hill and Longstreet and retreated for Henry Piper's older brother's house near the Potomac River.

The Piper Farm saw many couriers and soldiers come and go during the battle, and the site became a field hospital for the Confederacy, but the building never fell. After the battle, the Pipers returned to reclaim their land, which was soaked in bullets and blood.

Today the Piper Farmhouse is a quaint bed and breakfast that is said to be haunted by General Longstreet himself.

In the fall of 2001, 68-year-old Robert Janson and his wife were visiting Antietam as part of a tour they were taking of various Civil War sites. They became interested in the subject as part of a genealogy study they did where the couple learned they had distant relatives who actually fought in some of the battles. They hadn't heard of the Piper house being haunted until they arrived for the night—an overnight stay they will never forget. "When we got there we were chatting with the owner a little bit," Janson said. "The owner said, 'Well, you folks will be the only ones at the farmhouse tonight. There are no other guests.' I think they have maybe four or five rooms available, but we were the only ones at that particular time and he said, 'You'll be by yourself and we'll give you the big bedroom upstairs in the original part of the house. Here's the keys, we'll meet you in the morning,' and he left. We were by ourselves in the place. He told us to check out the guest book up there in the bedroom, and he said we'll see some very interesting things noted by other people who've been here in the past.

"Later on when I was reading through this thing, I see all these notations about people saying they saw Ole Pete, which was General Longstreet's nickname. All these entries suggested that we'll probably run into Pete. We figured, well, this should be interesting. So the owner left and we kind of toured around through the house that evening and so on, and then it was time to hit the sack and go to bed. My wife said she noticed in this guest book that a lot of the people mentioned that they had these occurrences about 1 AM. I said, 'Yeah, that's right.' And it was maybe about 12, 12:30, something like that. So we were in bed, but we hadn't gone to sleep yet when we heard this god-awful screaming outside of the house. We never heard anything like this. It sounded like a man in mortal pain—as if someone were running very fast from the front of the house and went around to the side. We jumped up and tried to look out this one side window, but we couldn't see a thing. Then we went and looked out the back where there was a cornfield, but we still couldn't see what it was, and the sound kind of disappeared into the night. My wife said, 'My god, I've never heard such a thing like this. Like someone was just running for their life.' It was a terrible, terrible scream."

The Jansons went back to their bedroom and locked the door. Soon Mrs. Janson drifted off to sleep, but Robert was a little restless. "Suddenly, downstairs in the first floor of this place I heard this crash," he said. "Have you ever heard someone take a door and slam it closed as hard as they can and you hear the crash of the door? Well, that's what it was. It sounded exactly like that. It kind of reverberated through the house. I look over there at the bedside clock and sure enough it was 1 AM.

"The sound woke my wife up and we're waiting to see what's going to happen now. We're thinking, good God, here comes Ole Pete. We heard noises downstairs and it seemed to be almost like someone walking up the steps on the stairway and coming up to our bedroom. But then it ended. And I didn't get to sleep until about an hour or two after that. The following morning we went downstairs. They had sent a housekeeper to cook breakfast for us. We mentioned this to the woman and she said, 'Oh, you heard Old Pete. That was definitely him.'"

After breakfast, Janson and his wife went outside to take some pictures of the property before they left. "We walked around the outside of the farmhouse and I took some pictures, one with my wife sitting on the front steps of this place, one looking at the house on the side, and another shot of my wife looking at the barn way down to the entrance to the driveway. It turns out that none of the pictures looking at the house came out. Only the shot looking toward the barn, away from the house, turned out fine. It was a weird experience and just kind of tied everything up."

There is a phenomenon that occurs with haunted historic locations. If you've ever traveled in the region surrounding Washington, D.C., there are many inns and bed and breakfasts that post a plaque reading "George Washington Slept Here." Some of these historic lodges also have haunted reputations, and more than a few of them claim their ghost is that of the United States' first president. Often, if there is any supernatural activity at all, such as disembodied voices or footsteps, or strange cold spots, those who live or work inside these possibly-haunted buildings will identify the ghost as the most famous person who ever even visited the site. Some of these locations may, indeed, be haunted by someone from the past, but saying an old inn is "haunted by a gardener who worked here for two weeks in the 1890s and slipped off the roof to his death" is not nearly as romantic as saying it is "haunted by the ghost of George Washington who slept here one night in 1779."

What makes the Piper Farmhouse different than many other sites who attach famous names to their knocks and disembodied murmuring voices is that some guests of the Piper have actually seen an apparition they knew to be Longstreet (or "Ole Pete" as those who work there now call him). The guest books in the rooms have several written accounts of seeing Longstreet, and in a couple of cases, some guests reported speaking to the General himself. They claimed Ole Pete was looking for Mary Ellen Piper. Perhaps he's still looking out for her safety, or maybe Ole Pete wants another glass of wine. Considering his distinguished military career and his post-war duties working with and for his former adversaries, he's certainly earned a drink.

# 14

# GETTYSBURG

**War:** United States Civil War (1861–1865)
**Dates of battle:** July 1–3, 1863
**Location:** Gettysburg, Pennsylvania
**Participation:** 97,000-man Union Army of the Potomac under General George G. Meade against 75,000-man Confederate Army of Northern Virginia under General Robert E. Lee.
**Casualties:** Over 51,000

*[W]e can not dedicate, we can not consecrate, we can not hallow this ground. The brave men, living and dead, who struggled here, have consecrated it, far above our poor power to add or detract. The world will little note, nor long remember what we say here, but it can never forget what they did here.*
—President Abraham Lincoln, excerpt from the "Gettysburg Address," November 19, 1863

In the database of our collective psyche, we simply cannot cross-reference "ghosts" and "war" without seeing one word at the top of the list: Gettysburg. Certainly there have been no bloodier three days in American history, and only the weapons of mass destruction the United States dropped on Hiroshima and Nagasaki, Japan, during World War II rival the loss of life in such a short time period during an act of war.

But the destruction of Hiroshima and Nagasaki took only minutes with the aid of a single atomic weapon dropped on each. Gettysburg's carnage was brought with cannons, muskets, pistols, swords, and even bare hands at times. Today the impressions, the history, and the ghosts are all that remain of the carnage.

For the Union Army of the North, Gettysburg was a critical victory considering their recent losses at the battles of Fredericksburg, Virginia, on December 13, 1862, and Chancellorsville, Virginia, May 1–5, 1863. At both battles, Confederate General Robert E. Lee outmaneuvered his Union opponents, though the North initially held the upper hand in each conflict. Lee left the Northern Army humiliated. In early summer of 1863, General Lee proposed to the Confederate government that an invasion and victory in Pennsylvania—on enemy soil—would break the back of the Union Army, bring an armistice, and, ultimately, Southern independence. But Gettysburg was not the predetermined site for this historic and potentially war-ending battle to take place. So how did the infamous battle get here?

It must have been the shoes.

In the first two weeks of June 1863, the Confederate Army—now divided into three corps by General Lee—moved north through Virginia, across the Potomac River, into Maryland, and then Pennsylvania where they raided and plundered the livestock, food, shoes, and other supplies from towns they encountered along the route. The Southern troops were so in need of basic supplies that their tattered and torn uniforms, swollen and callused feet, and partially emaciated physiques made certain units look like the army of the undead. They were fighting to be free of the Union, but as they invaded deeper into the North, they also fought for their very survival. Word of the invasion spread quickly to the Union Army in the south, who raced home with renewed vigor as their homeland was now being invaded. For the Union Army, there was an opportunity to cut off the Confederates from their home base and finish them off in Pennsylvania. Both sides were betting the war on this invasion. General Joseph Hooker, who led the Union Army, was panicked at the thought of taking on General Lee's army that currently outnumbered his own. President Lincoln knew Hooker was no longer the man to lead the Union soldiers, so he accepted Hooker's resignation on June 28. Major General George Gordon Meade was promoted (much to his surprise, considering he was fourth commander of the Army of the Potomac and others had more seniority) because of his impressive record as division commander and his superior tactical skills.

Meade and his men were heading into southern Pennsylvania and were in a position to potentially separate two of Lee's Confederate Corps and strand the southern army in the north. On June 28, Lee learned of the Union Army position and progress from a spy—he immediately sent scouts to amass his divisions.

So what about the shoes? The legend says that Confederate Major General Henry Heth and his division marched toward Gettysburg on June 29 because he was chasing an alleged mass supply of shoes in town for his men. Historians point out that Gettysburg had only a few shoemakers—no more or less than any other town of that size (Gettysburg's population was approximately 2,400 people in 1863)—and there was never a large supply of shoes. But the shoe story may still hold, because it is possible Heth may have used the shoe excuse after the battle was over as his reasoning for charging into an enemy position and starting a battle that handed a devastating loss to the South. But Heth marched his men into the sights of John Buford's Union cavalry division, who had arrived the day before on word the Confederate Army was marching close by. Buford decided Gettysburg's hills and ridges offered the best position to hold off his enemy, so he sent word to Major General John Reynolds, who was commander of the Union Army's first infantry division in Emmitsburg, Maryland. Buford called for the reinforcements and in doing so determined the epic battle would be fought in Gettysburg.

On July 1, Lieutenant Marcellus Jones of the 8th Illinois Cavalry, Company E fired the first shot at Heth's Confederate marching mass of gray. Lt. Jones retreated to Buford's front line on Herr Ridge and the battle was on.

By the end of July 3, more than 11,000 soldiers were killed, 10,000 more were either missing in action or captured, and 29,000 were wounded. Confederate casualties are estimated between 25,000 and 28,000 and Union casualties totaled 23,000. The streams near the battle-fields literally ran crimson with the blood of the dead and wounded. The battle was one that could never be forgotten; historians, preservationists, and the myriad of ghosts insist on that.

*The aftermath of Gettysburg.*
*Photos courtesy of the Library of Congress*

Ghosts have become synonymous with Gettysburg. Sightings have occurred for more than a century. Many have heard of people spotting phantom divisions of Civil War soldiers marching through Devil's Den or the Wheatfield. The witness assumes they're seeing some kind of reenactment that so often takes place in Gettysburg—but the division soon disappears.

One of the more predominant locations for sightings is at Iverson's Pits. It was at a stone wall on the side of Doubleday Avenue where Brigadier General Henry Baxter and his brigade stopped an entire North Carolina brigade led by General Alfred Iverson. Hundreds of Confederate soldiers were cut down before they could advance on the Union brigade. The fallen were buried in a mass grave at a nearby farm field that became known as Iverson's Pits. In 1873, the mass grave was exhumed by a Confederate memorial association who took the remains to North Carolina for reburial. Locals insist the association didn't (and likely couldn't) find the remains of everyone, and every year on July 1, the ghosts of those who weren't taken home to North Carolina rise from Iverson's Pits and march the fields before disappearing into the ether. But ghost sightings here don't only happen on July 1.

On September 5, 2000, then-38-year-old David Hoover was visiting Gettysburg for four days. He made a stop on a self-guided tour at Iverson's Pits around 1:45 PM and even recalls what he was wearing—a khaki baseball cap, gray shirt, and blue shorts—potentially looking similar to either Union or Confederate at a quick glance. I spoke to Hoover about his experience there. "After passing through the barrier of several feet of cornstalks, I reached a wide-open field," he said. "I looked over at the cornfield to my left several yards away and I noticed an area that was only sporadically strewn with corn, and I headed in that direction."

Once Hoover arrived at the clearing, he said he saw some of the corn stalks wavering in front of him. At first he thought it was the wind or some animal, but soon he saw something else. "I put my camera to my eye to take a photo," he said. "As I looked through my viewfinder, I saw two black objects side-by-side. I lowered my camera to make sure it wasn't something on my lens, but there they were—about 20–30 feet away in the middle of the clearing. I took one step backward with my right foot; as soon as it touched the open field behind me, the two objects seemed to grow in size, as if they were coming in my direction. I fumbled with my camera, and as I did, the two objects seemed to turn quickly outward, as if back-to-back."

He explained how the two black objects shrunk again and then disappeared into the underbrush. "Just seconds after they had started moving, I could hear the sound of rustling leaves on the ground and the hitting of the stalks in the direction of where the objects went." But this wasn't the end of Hoover's unexplained experience at Gettysburg.

Shaken after the initial encounter, Hoover laughed out of relief, then snapped a picture of Iverson's Pits before heading back to his car, being careful to watch for animals in case some critter had stirred the cornstalks earlier. He said, "I began to walk back parallel to the field to where I had initially entered. After one or two steps, I noticed something in the corn out of the corner of my eye. I turned and looked, and it was the figure of a soldier moving parallel with me. He was perhaps 20 feet away. I immediately stopped. He kept going, accelerating and gliding as he went on his way to where my only access back to my car was. He was wearing a full-brimmed hat and looked like he had a knapsack on, and he was holding a rifle at port-arms. His color was mostly black, but a grayish-blue seemed to come and go as he moved. The same happened with his outline—at times it was full, then it would nearly disappear, then would grow back to full-size. I could hear him hitting the stalks, not just as a man walking or running through them, but as loud as a man swinging at them with a baseball bat. All of this time, not a single stalk was moved or stirred by him gliding through them. The sound was as if someone were chopping them down. Because it also sounded as if it was strong enough to take a person's head off, I ducked my head down and away, and said, 'Relax, man!' At this point, I had forgotten about my camera, an error which I regret to this day. I may also have been subconsciously wary of possible reprisals from this apparition at having his picture taken. It might have been 20 or 30 seconds until this figure finally disappeared. I crouched down and looked into the stalks and thought I could see bluish-gray trousers with a wide, white stripe down the side. They were untucked and hung freely on top of black shoes. This part may have been my imagination, because the image was gone as quickly as I had seen it."

Hoover figured the specter was one of the fallen Confederate soldiers, so he announced to the presence that he was in fact born in North Carolina and now lived in Florida. He was having trouble finding his path through the tall corn stalks and back to his car, so he asked for help. "I said, 'Will you let me pass?'" He said, "A few seconds later, I heard that rustling sound again to my right, as the corn leaves near me moved. Then it stopped. I paused, then made my decision; I spoke out, 'I'm coming through. Hold your fire.' About halfway through, I lost my way along the broken path, and while looking for it, I was also glancing to my right, hoping that the swinging sounds and the force behind it wouldn't come back. I soon found it, made it to the marker, and as I walked slowly into the clearing between the corn, I said back over my right shoulder, 'Thank you.' I didn't panic, but once I reached the 88th Pennsylvania Monument, I sat at its base for about 30 minutes to collect myself. I kept looking at the ground and then to the corn where I had seen it all, trying to make some sense of it."

For David Hoover, Gettysburg offered him one of the most profound experiences of his life. He practically touched history. Iverson's Pits is by no means the only hot spot in town. Sachs Bridge is another supernaturally active location.

Built in 1854 by David Spooner, the bridge was commissioned at a cost of $1,544 and was originally called Sauck's Bridge. The 100-foot covered bridge crosses Marsh Creek and connects the Townships of Cumberland and Freedom, and it served as a critical retreat route for half of Robert E. Lee's army on July 3 and 4 as the Southern army filed out. But the bridge also has a darker side—three men were hung from the rafters of the bridge, and a field hospital where many wounded soldiers drew their last breath was also nearby—lending to the ghostly reputation the area has now.

Today, the red-painted covered bridge is a quaint image set across the water and at the edge of the woods. Only foot traffic is allowed to cross the historic landmark now. The clip-clop of horses and the metallic grind of wagon wheels is long gone, but certainly not forgotten.

In the early morning hours of Saturday, May 8, 2004, Stacey Jones, founder of Central New York Ghost Hunters, and members of her group were visiting Sachs Bridge as part of a Gettysburg ghost investigation. I spoke to her about her experiences there. She described the night as unseasonably warm considering it was early May, and the night was clear, but that quickly changed. "All of a sudden this fog came in," Jones said. "And then we started seeing lights."

"What kind of lights?" I asked.

"They were coming from the field across from Sachs Bridge. These orange lights were coming from the ground and going up in an arch about 12 feet in the air and then coming back down again. That went on for quite a while in this fog. We stood there and watched it and then we started hearing horses [she imitated the nasally, lip-flapping sigh of a horse] and then we started hearing rumbles—the only way I can describe it is like a cannon being shot from far away. That lasted about 20 minutes, and then the fog disappeared and everything stopped."

Stacey and her team returned to Sachs Bridge around 10 PM that same day and had a second encounter. After an hour of taking photographs, video, and trying to obtain spirit voices on audio tape, Jones and six others from her group sat on the stone wall that separates Sachs Bridge from the open field where they witnessed the strange lights the night before. She felt that sitting quietly offered the best opportunity for experiencing something supernatural. Her hunch would soon be proven correct. "We turned everything off and the only thing we had going were tape recorders," she said. "After about 15 minutes I started seeing shadows in the field—they were between 5 and 6 feet tall and they were moving in the grass. Then one of my other people piped up and said, 'Do you see those shadows?' And I figured, OK, it's not just me. So we stood there watching this and then the lights started again—the lights were arching from the grass. Meanwhile, this cold came in—it had to be in the high 70s that night but that cold made it feel like 30 or 40 degrees. And the cold would come in and then leave and then come in again. Then everybody else except me started to smell flowers. So people are smelling flowers, we're watching the shadows and seeing the lights, and then it got quiet again.

There were no more shadow people and no more lights, but we heard men's voices out in the field."

"Could you hear what they were saying?" I asked.

"We couldn't make out what they were saying; all we could tell was that they were male voices. And we could hear movement in the tree line. At this point I thought someone was out there trying to mess with us, so one of my people went out and walked out there with a flashlight, but there was nobody there. The voices came right up beside us on the tree line and then things got quiet and we started hearing the horses again. The horses were coming from the other side of the bridge, and then we heard a growl right behind us where the water was—it sounded like a man growling. I turned and said to my people, 'Did you hear that?' And someone in my group said, 'What, that growl?' And we hit the ground running and we jumped in our van to leave."

The aftermath of the battle at Gettysburg was hellish. Bodies, spent weapons, and carnage were strewn everywhere. Tillie Pierce was 15 years old at the time of the battle, and she published her memoir of the battle 26 years later. On July 5, 1863, Tillie and some of her friends went to Little Round Top to survey the post-battle field. She wrote:

*As we stood upon those mighty boulders, and looked down into the chasms between, we beheld the dead lying there just as they had fallen during the struggle. From the summit of Little Round Top, surrounded by the wrecks of battle, we gazed upon the valley of death beneath. The view there spread out before us was terrible to contemplate! It was an awful spectacle! Dead soldiers, bloated horses, shattered cannon and caissons, thousands of small arms. In fact everything belonging to army equipments was there in one confused and indescribable mass.*

The ghosts who haunt Gettysburg came from the south and they came from the north. Brothers and kin were locked in mortal battle against one another in the once-quiet fields of this rural town. Their spirits have proven President Lincoln correct—we never will forget what they did here, where they walked, and why they died.

# 15

# KENNESAW MOUNTAIN BATTLEFIELD

**War:** United States Civil War (1861–1865)
**Dates of Battle:** May 23–July 2, 1864
**Location:** Kennesaw, Georgia
**Participants:** 100,000-man Union Army under
General William Tecumseh Sherman against 67,000-man
Confederate Army under General Joseph Eggleston Johnston
**Casualties:** Over 4,000

*An order came at six o'clock this morning that our artillery would open on the enemy, and that our infantry should hug their breastworks closely, so as to be protected from the enemy's fire of shot and shell . . . About five o'clock, artillery began to play slowly, and soon firing became brisk. It was said that the 4th and 14th Corps were to assail the enemy's works, and the appearances were decidedly as though there would be a big battle today.*
—Major Fredrick C. Winkler,
26th Wisconsin Infantry, June 27, 1864

General William Sherman was on a tear through Georgia. His objective was to march straight through the supply stronghold of Atlanta, down to the coast, and break the back of the Confederate Army in the process. But to reach Atlanta, Sherman would first have to face a dug-in Confederate army that was determined to stop the North troops from invading any further. Confederate troops set up their pickets on Lost Mountain, and from there they'd make their stand.

The name Kennesaw comes from the Cherokee Indian "Gah-nee-sah" which means burial ground—an ominous name that would certainly earn its moniker when the North and South clashed here in 1864.

"Battle of Kenesaw (sic) Mountain" by Kurz & Allison,
c1891, courtesy of the Library of Congress (LC-USZC4-1766)

When Misha Kantartzis and her family moved to Marietta, Georgia, in June of 2000, they weren't Civil War buffs. They knew there were battles fought in the region, but that was about it. Prior to renting a house on the corner of Route 120 (Dallas Highway) and Casteel Road, they had never experienced anything supernatural either. Misha, her husband, and her four children would soon find that the world of the United States Civil War and the world of ghosts had converged on the property they now called home, causing them to quickly learn a few things about both subjects.

The house, built in the 1870s, offered views of both Kennesaw and the Lost Mountains, and was, at one point, used during the Kennesaw Mountain Civil War campaign, though the Kantartzises didn't know it at the time. "We started noticing strange things right away," Mischa Kantartzis said. "I just chalked it up to being a new home and not being familiar with the sounds and things like that.

"My husband and I don't smoke in the house, so we would always go out on the back porch to smoke and it seemed like every time I was out there, it just felt like somebody was watching me. It's really hard to describe it, but it was just that feeling. That's how things actually started. I'd say within a two-week period, my husband was out of town working, the kids were getting ready for school, and I was busy unpacking. I was in my dining room, and I had seen what looked like a general. I wasn't really familiar with anything with the Confederacy or the Union other than knowing when the Civil War happened. But this man was in a blue uniform. I saw him clear as a bell. It kind of shocked me. He was 2 feet from me, and it was full figure, too. I noticed the emblems that he had on the shoulders—that's what led me to believe he was a general because of what he was wearing. He was definitely in charge. But the thing was, he wasn't aware of me. Almost like I was watching a movie or something. He seemed to be real agitated like he was barking out orders or something— that was the impression I got. He was gone within a matter of seconds."

"Did you tell anyone about it?" I asked.

"I told my husband about it. I said, 'There's something odd about this house,' and I told him it was really weird, he [the General's ghost] was just there for a second, and then he was gone. We didn't say anything to any of the kids because we didn't want to spook them or anything."

"What other kinds of things were happening there?" I asked.

"It was probably the third month we were there," she said. "I was mopping the wooden floors. The house was originally a two-family setup. The one family lived upstairs and the mother-in-law lived downstairs, so there's a full kitchen, living room, bathroom, bedroom, and everything downstairs. I was mopping down that hallway and there's a window that sits right at the foot of the stairs, and someone had put a mirror up on the wall right next to where the window was so you could look in the mirror and see out the window.

"As I was mopping, something caught my eye—some kind of movement. We had no pets or anything at that time, so I was kind of curious as to what was out there. When I looked in the mirror, I saw what had to be hundreds of legs marching by. It was really weird because they were above where the ground level actually was, so it was almost like they were marching through air. They were 2 or 3 feet from the ground, so I figure the elevation must have been different at the time of the battle."

"You could only see their legs?" I asked.

"Because of the way the window was, I could only see the legs. I stood there for a minute, and I was trying to convince myself I wasn't seeing it.

My immediate thought was to contact the owner and see if they had experienced anything strange, but then I was like, well, I don't want them to think we were crazy [*laughs*]. Then I went upstairs. That's the point when the whole family got together and started talking."

Everyone in Misha's family was afraid to talk about what they were experiencing in that house, but once she came forward to share what was happening to her, others in her family related similar accounts. "My daughter had actually seen a Confederate soldier," Kantartzis said. "I don't know if he was a prisoner or if he was wounded, but he seemed to manifest more down on the lower part of the house where her room was. There were two definite spirits, I guess you'd call them, that were there. I know one was the general that I saw, and then there was one downstairs. I never saw him, but I had a really creepy feeling. I mean he was very scary. We always got the feeling that he was just very angry."

After the ghost encounters were out in the open, Misha took a trip to the Kennesaw Mountain Battlefield National Park, which was just a few miles from her house. She knew what she saw and experienced in her house, but she didn't know much about the battles that took place in the region and wanted to learn more.

In the spring of 1864, Union Army Commander-in-Chief General Ulysses S. Grant ordered his armies to go on the offensive and drive south. Atlanta was the objective. If the Union could sack Atlanta, they would disrupt the major railroad hub there, pilfer Confederate storage facilities, and put a nail in the coffin that was the Civil War.

Union Gen. Sherman was trying to flank Confederate Gen. Johnston by heading southwest, then looping around behind his forces in order to hold Atlanta. From May 4 to May 23, 1864, the two armies played a cat-and-mouse game from Chattanooga, Tennessee, down through northwestern Georgia.

Gen. Johnston knew he couldn't win an all-out assault on a level battleground. The Southern troops were significantly outnumbered and outgunned. The Union forces totaled 100,000 men, 254 cannons, and 35,000 horses, while Johnston's army had 63,000 soldiers and only 187 cannons. Gen. Johnston took positions and waited for the Union advance. But a small skirmish ensued, and he retreated his forces to take up a new position further south. What the Union army didn't know was that Gen. Johnston was buying time while units dug trenches and pickets in the vicinity of Kennesaw and the Lost Mountain just outside of Marietta, Georgia.

Johnston was setting up a protective arc around Marietta and Atlanta where they could make a last stand. If Atlanta fell, the end would be nigh for the Confederacy. Plus, the Western and Atlantic Railroad track ran near Kennesaw Mountain—a lifeline that had to be protected for the South to stay in the war.

On May 23, 1864, Johnston's troops entered the Kennesaw Mountain region and took up their elevated positions. By holding the high ground in the mountains, the Confederates hoped Sherman would send waves of forces up the hills in a futile attempt to overthrow the rebel forces. Early on, Gen. Johnston's plan was working. Between May 23 and June 27, Sherman engaged his troops in various skirmishes along the hilly front. During the skirmishes, Union casualties were nearly three times as high as the dug-in Confederates, giving southern forces hope that their position would hold.

After weeks of skirmishes, a standoff was coming to a head between the two sides. From their Kennesaw mountaintop lookout, Confederates could also watch Union troop movements. When Sherman made his move to try and flank a division south around the mountains, Johnston responded by shifting some 11,000 men under Lt. Gen. John Bell Hood to block. Hood clashed with Federal forces at Kolb's Farm on June 22. It would be a costly encounter. The Confederates were betting on Gen. Sherman assuming they would take up defensive positions, so instead they attacked. Some recent rain had left swollen swamps and streams, and footing was treacherous on the day of the attack. The Union soldiers held the road near the farm while the South fought through swamp and underbrush. By nightfall, more than 1,000 Confederate soldiers were lost, compared with about 350 Union soldiers. The South claimed victory because they were able to drive the Yankees back to their reserve line. The Confederates held their line, though the front was now 8 miles long and getting more difficult to manage.

The morning of June 27 began with the thunder of Union cannons. The objective was to soften the Confederate defenses before foot soldiers stormed the front lines. This plan mostly backfired, as the cannons inflicted little damage to the well-bunkered Confederates, but the sounds did alert every person within many miles that today would be the attack. After 15 minutes, the cannons stopped and Union forces charged against a waiting rebel army. In the area of Noyes Creek, the first confrontation occurred. Union infantry collided with the 63rd Georgia Regiment. Hand-to-hand fighting and a bullet fest followed, driving the rebels back to their own reserve line. As the Union forces drew closer, the Confederates waiting behind the reserve line opened up on them, pushing them back.

At Cheatham Hill, Gen. Sherman decided to send 8,000 soldiers in a blue wave up the hill toward two of Gen. Johnston's finest commanders and their men. The hope was to break through the line and rout the Confederates from all sides. Hundreds of Union boys and men became easy targets for cannons and gunfire. The Confederate line held, and the Federal forces retreated to safer ground.

Gen. Sherman would give up on the idea of taking the mountain region and go the long way around if he must—an inevitable move that forced Gen. Johnston to also withdraw from the mountains on July 2 and head for Atlanta for a final effort to save the city, the state, and the South.

Cheatham Hill is another paranormal hotspot. Harold "Pappy" Harmon is a Civil War reenactor with the 28th Georgia and 123rd New York Volunteer Infantry. His organization has members who portray both Federal and Confederate soldiers, and they travel to various battlefield sites throughout the United States. He and his group were visiting the Kennesaw Battlefields on June 26, 2000, which happened to be on the anniversary of one of the battles.

"We were camped out there very close to Cheatham Hill and back toward the Texas monument," Harmon said. "And we decided to go haint huntin' ['haint' is a southern word for ghost or haunt]. So a group of us went out around midnight; there were several of us and a young boy that was 11 or 12 years old. When we got to a certain area of the trail, about three or four of the guys ran off in the woods and just went crazy hollerin' and just seemed to be absolutely out of their minds and I couldn't keep up with them. I stayed with the boy. We went back to the Illinois monument and spent some time up there and then we started back to our camp. By this time it was really dark. We were walking back and we had this big lantern, and one of them had the bright idea to put the lantern out. So we put it out and this is when the boy started seeing the ghosts. This was in an area of the trail where the actual battle of Cheatham Hill was fought."

Harmon went on to describe the conditions of the area back in late June of 1864. Cheatham Hill hadn't received much rain, and the grasses and field were dry and brittle. With all of the ordinance going back and forth, fires broke out in the field. Wounded men lay there and some were engulfed by flames, dying a more horrible death than the loss of blood would provide. One of the Confederate officers waved a white flag of truce so both sides could put out the fires, retrieve their wounded, and then get back to their battle.

"So the ghosts that the kid saw were burned," Pappy Harmon said. "He said, 'They're horrible, they're burned up, they're terrible-looking. He saw actual ghosts of the men after they had burned. I didn't see any of that, but it was at that part of the trail where this historical event happened."

"There was an eerie feeling, and that's about all I can say. It was so black that night. It was just pitch black—black as the inside of a Jefferson Brogan [*black leather shoes*]. I couldn't see the kid, but I could feel him quivering. You know how you have a feeling that something bad is going to happen? Well, that's the way I felt, so I tried to hurry him out of there. We went down the pathway with him hollering and carrying on, and finally at this point the trail bears to the left but also goes straight out to the road—so I got him out to the road and then he calmed down a little bit. If you enter from the paved road, at that point you'll see a marker that tells about the exact event with the men being caught in the brushfire and burning."

History often supports these ghost encounters. Harmon and his group's experience offers us a macabre glance back in time. And Misha Kantartzis's ghostly claim of living on a haunted property also has merit in the record books. "Union soldiers camped there for about three weeks in May and June of 1864," Kantartzis said. "I went to the Kennesaw Mountain National Battlefield Park—it was about a mile away from where the house was. When I was speaking to the curator, he was telling me that there were a lot of snipers in the trees that would sit and wait for the Union soldiers to move in."

Kantartzis learned from the curator that across the street from her house was a Union tent hospital where the Federals initially treated their wounded before shipping the stable patients back up to a hospital in Chattanooga. Where her house stood was a camp where Union forces stayed for three weeks—much of it unseasonably cold and rainy. All of these facts she learned after witnessing the ghost of an officer and a phantom regiment marching in her backyard.

Misha and her family moved out of the house in October 2003 and haven't experienced anything supernatural since. The house has since been torn down and is under commercial development.

# 16

# CARNTON PLANTATION– THE BATTLE OF FRANKLIN

**War:** United States Civil War (1861–1865)
**Date of battle:** November 30, 1864
**Location:** Franklin, Tennessee
**Participants:** 38,000 Union men under Major General John M. Schofield against 32,000 Confederate soldiers under General John B. Hood
**Casualties:** Over 9,500

*[Franklin] is the blackest page in the history of the War of the Lost Cause. It was the bloodiest battle of modern times in any war. It was the finishing stroke to the Independence of the Southern Confederacy. I was there. I saw it.*

—Sam Watkins, 1st Tennessee Infantry

Carnton Plantation didn't ask to become a Civil War site, it just happened. Duty called, and the McGavock family who owned the plantation answered. It was November 1864, and the Union army under Major General John Schofield was heading north to combine forces with the Army of the Cumberland just north of Nashville. Confederate General John Hood was determined to pick Schofield's army apart before they reached their comrades. On November 29, the two armies fought the Battle of Spring Hill where Hood failed to separate and destroy Schofield's divisions. This battle set the stage for the Battle of Franklin the following day—a battle that led to over 9,500 casualties on both sides combined. It was in the aftermath of this battle that the Carnton Plantation became a field hospital for the wounded and dying Confederate soldiers.

The Federal Army arrived in Franklin around 1 AM on November 29 and took up a defensive position on the southern end of town. The Union managed little sleep, as the night was spent preparing to fight. By 2 PM that afternoon, General Hood ordered a frontal assault even though one of his field commanders, General Cheatham, warned, "I don't like the looks of this fight, as the enemy has a good position and is well fortified." But Hood insisted, and his men said they would break the Union line or die trying. The Confederates marched into suicide. The fighting was hand-to-hand, and bayonets and clubs flew alongside the musket balls. Men clawed, stabbed, and choked each other at the front, but the Federal line held. The fighting went on for five hours and into nightfall. By midnight, the Union army retreated and headed for Nashville, but not before exacting a heavy toll on their enemy. Federal casualties totaled 2,500 while Confederate dead, wounded, and captured totaled over 7,000.

The Confederates picked up their hurt and dying and brought them to various field hospitals for medical attention. Many of the boys in gray found their way to the Carnton Plantation. Confederate Colonel W. D. Gale of General Stewart's Staff in the Army of Tennessee said of Mrs. McGavock's house and Carnton Plantation:

*The house is one of the large old-fashioned houses of the better class in Tennessee, two stories high, with many rooms. This was taken as a hospital, and the wounded, in hundreds, were brought to it during the battle, and all the night after. Every room was filled, every bed had two poor, bleeding fellows, every spare space, niche, and corner under the stairs, in the hall, everywhere— but one room for her own family. And when the noble old house could hold no more, the yard was appropriated until the wounded and the dead filled that, and all were not yet provided for.*

*Our doctors were deficient in bandages, and she began by giving her old linen, then her towels and napkins, then her sheets and tablecloths, then her husband's shirts and her own undergarments. During all this time the surgeons plied their dreadful work amid the sighs and moans and death rattle. Yet, amid it all, the noble woman was very active and constantly at work. During all the night neither she nor any of the household slept, but dispensed tea and coffee and such stimulants as she had, and that, too, with her own hands.*

On the Plantation property is another important relic of the Civil War and of the battle of Franklin: the McGavock Confederate Cemetery, where 1,481 Confederate soldiers who were killed at Franklin are buried, as are 15 veterans of the battle. The Battle of Franklin is not forgotten at Carnton Plantation today.

Gary Lima is a 53-year-old Civil War reenactor from Tennessee, something he's been doing since 2000. He's a former Marine Sergeant, and for his day job he works as a supervisor in the Tennessee Emergency Management Agency's fixed nuclear facilities—meaning he's got security clearance well beyond most of us and he's been vetted by quite a few government agencies. "I like telling the story about the Confederate soldiers," Lima said. "They were real, they had wives, and they had children, and they suffered. That should be remembered." Lima used to scoff at talk of the paranormal, but a few experiences at the Carnton Plantation made him change his views a little bit.

In May 2002, Lima brought his horse and his Confederate gear to the plantation to put on a children's program one Saturday. He was invited to spend the night on the property, and because there was some wind and rain in the air, he and his friend Kane Rubalcaba were allowed to sleep on the back porch of the main house to offer them some cover from the weather. "We put together what we call a shebang, which is a canvas over some chairs and long benches, and we built ourselves a little place to sleep during the night," Lima said. "The next morning we were going to ride from there in our Confederate Calvary impression and be in the rodeo parade."

That evening, before Lima and Rubalcaba turned in for the night, a friend of Rubalcaba's named Marty Luffman came over to bring them some dinner. Luffman, a State Farm insurance agent from Smyrna, was into photography and clicked some pictures of the house and the property while he was there. During the early evening, a few strange events happened to Lima—nothing he would have paid much attention to had it not been for something that would happen to him a few hours later, in the dead of night.

While driving his truck down near the cemetery to pick up some campfire wood, the windshield wiper on his truck broke off so he stopped to fix it. "And then my friend Kane said, 'You know, somebody's on the back bumper of your truck pushing it up and down,'" Lima said. "I went back there, but there's nobody there. So I'm kind of laughing it off because I don't believe in the paranormal per se. The camera guy who's been doing amateur photos for years said, 'That's really strange. There's some cold spots and some warm spots around here,' and he showed us where. I said, 'What does that mean?' He said, 'Well, that means there's some-body here and we just can't see 'em.' I didn't want to be rude [laughs] but I thought, 'You're a little flaky,' but I didn't say anything. So we brought the firewood back, and then Marty left so it was just Kane and me."

Lima and Rubalcaba tied their horses up to a picket line not far from the house, went to bed in their makeshift tent, and tried to get some sleep on the hard plank-wood flooring of the porch. "We were awakened by a noise and my buddy Kane says, 'Gary, my horse is gone.' So immediately we're thinking a horse is gone, we've got a subdivision not far away, we've got to get a hold of that animal. So we jumped up and went to check on my horse and saw that he was still tied up. Kane went and found his horse, he wasn't too far away, and brought him back. But it was the strangest thing; the horse got free, there's the halter, there's the lead, but the lead is balled up. Kane's horse had a cotton lead, and it was balled up like yarn that a cat has been playing with. I'd never seen anything like it, and he'd never seen anything like it. It took him forever to get that thing undone."

What happened next will stay with Gary Lima forever. The two men managed to get to sleep on the floor after securing the horses, but around three in the morning, Lima was awakened again. He found that his feet were resting across Rubalcaba's feet at a 45-degree angle, which was strange considering he would have had to shift considerably in the night for his feet to get into that position, and for neither man to wake up from that seemed peculiar. But Lima thought this could be chalked up to something just shy of sleepwalking. Then he heard something out in the cemetery. "I heard children's sounds," he said. "And I'm thinking that there are kids in the Confederate cemetery playing. I get a little upset at that because that whole area there is the preservation area. I'm suddenly thinking that some teenagers or kids from the subdivision are in that cemetery messing around.

"Now, that cemetery is sacred ground. That's disrespectful and I'm thinking maybe they don't know any better or maybe some parents can't control their kids, I don't know. I roll over and look down at the cemetery. In between the clouds there was some light coming through, and I didn't see any kids playing. And as I'm rolling over I hear kids inside the house now on the opposite end from where we are lying on the deck. They're laughing. They sounded like kids—maybe not even teenagers yet—and I heard the sounds of their feet running through the house to where we were. I'm going, 'Now wait a minute. The front door is locked, we're here in the back. How could these kids have gotten inside the house? And who would be doing this at 3 o'clock in the morning anyway?'

"As I'm rolling over and trying to figure it out, I look in the window and there's a little girl looking at me and what looks like a little boy down below with his hands on the windowsill, but I'm seeing her. And she's kind of laughing, making merry, like a little prankster—like a little girl up to something. And I make this comment to myself: 'They must've been pretty nice kids back then.' Then I go to sleep."

Lima took a sidebar here to tell me about his years in the Marines where he saw some pretty tough situations. "I know what it's like to have sleep deprivation," he said. The week before seeing the little girl in the window was a tough one for him. He did a lot of work to prepare for the living history program, and now he was sleeping on the wood planks of a back porch. He figured he was overtired and his mind was playing tricks on him. So he went back to sleep. He didn't give the little girl much more thought until a month or so later when Rubalcaba told him he had to give his photographer friend, Marty Luffman, a call right away. Lima said, "So I called and Marty said, 'Gary, you're not going to believe it.' He said there's pictures of what he called orbs that he took when we were down in the cemetery area when we got the firewood, and then he said, 'Gary, there's a picture of a little girl looking out a window.' I said, 'Marty, I thought I was dreaming.' He asked me what I meant. I told him what happened at three in the morning. He said he had taken these photographs the day before in the evening before we left.

"I asked him, 'Does she have blondish hair and a round face?' And he said, 'Yeah.'"

Luffman took his photographs to the *Tennessean*, Nashville's major daily newspaper and had their photo experts take a look at the photo. "It wasn't a forgery," Lima said. He and Rubalcaba went back to Carnton Plantation to get a tour of the inside of the house with a reporter. "I'd never been in the house until after I saw the photo," Lima said. "We went upstairs during our tour because somebody said there's a picture of the kids upstairs and there was this oil painting, and there's that girl in the oil painting."

"Did you recognize the girl?" I asked.

"That's when I realized that the girl in the oil painting was the same girl I saw. The girl was McGavock's daughter who died as a young girl. I didn't know that. The boy apparently died, too."

The painting Lima saw was that of Mary Elizabeth McGavock. Mary was just 9 years old when she died of an unknown illness in 1858—just a few years before the Battle of Franklin came roaring into her backyard. Two other paintings of the McGavock children were also in the room: Martha Winder, who died of heart disease at age 12, and John Randal McGavock, who was only 3 months old when he died but was painted to look older in his "death portrait."

*Could this be Mary Elizabeth McGavock in the lower-right corner of the window to the right of the door?*
*Photo by Marty Luffman, Nashville, Tennessee*

I spoke with Marty Luffman about this photograph that made regional and even national news programs back in 2002. Luffman believes he captured the spirit image of young Mary Elizabeth—the very same girl Gary Lima saw in the window that same weekend. He also believes some of the spirits of Carnton Plantation may have followed him home to Georgia. "The children came home with me, and so did the woman," Luffman said. "It got almost out of hand at my house. When they blessed the house, we could hear the children crying, they didn't want to leave. But the woman stayed. And I've hollered at her. She's broken four large mirrors in my house that were hanging on the wall. I call her Mrs. McGavock, I don't know if that's her or not, but I call her that. I said, 'Break one more mirror and I'm going to kick your butt [*laughs*].' These things are costing me $100, $150 apiece. And you know what she did right after that? I have a mirror upstairs that hangs on the wall—it probably weighs 125 pounds—it came off the wall out in the middle of the floor and didn't break. There wasn't a scratch on it, but it was loud."

Gary Lima no longer scoffs at claims of the supernatural. And he has an appreciation for what the bigger implications of his experiences are. Lima says he's a Christian, and he doesn't believe what he experienced is counter to any of the religious teachings he's experienced in his faith. "If I said this didn't happen to protect my reputation, I would be a liar," he said. "It's more important I not be a liar. I don't care what the world says. I saw it, I heard it, and I physically experienced it. The people who lived in that house are part of the foundation of our country. We need to consider the lives that were lived there. It's not just about the soldiers, we need to think about the families. When these men came home, guess who was waiting there for them? The women and children."

Seeing the ghost of Mary Elizabeth McGavock wasn't Lima's last brush with the unexplained at Carnton Plantation. The year after his first experience at Carnton, he had another, this time in the Confederate Cemetery on the property. He said, "One November we were doing a living history program for the weekend, and we did a micro-scale version of the Battle of Franklin for everyone. My buddy Kane and I were going through the cemetery to go to his truck to get some stuff. It was dark, the moon was out, and there was this cold blanket of fog coming in and out—it was pretty neat. The fog wasn't very high, it was just blanketing the ground. We're going through the cemetery and some guy passed us from behind wearing a Confederate officer's uniform, and we didn't recognize him. He was kind of pale-looking, like he hadn't been outside and weathered like we were. He had his hands behind his back. He was a young-looking Confederate officer in a pristine uniform, and we're just not that pristine. Even the Confederate reenacting officers, their uniforms look good, but they don't look *that* good. He had a sullen appearance like he was kind of downtrodden and he just walked past us quietly. We said hello to him but he didn't say anything, which is somewhat rude. This guy went past us like he'd come out of the cleaners, then he disappeared through the fog and went out the front gate.

"Then it hits us when we get to the truck. Kane goes, 'Gary, each time we opened up the gate you can hear the iron gate slam.' I said, 'Yeah, so . . . what's up?' He said, 'When he passed us, you didn't hear the gates open or the gate slam.' I didn't recognize the fellow. We checked with our infantry reenactors there, we went by their campfires, and nobody saw the guy we described.

"I said to Kane, 'Look, after the experience on the back deck, I'm just glad we're wearing the right uniform [*laughs*].'"

# 17

# ANDERSONVILLE PRISON

**War:** United States Civil War (1861–1865)
**Dates of operation:** February 1864–May 1865
**Location:** Andersonville, Sumter County, Georgia
**Participants:** Fort Sumter was a Confederate prison under
Southern Captain Henry Wirz, Commandant.
The fort was designed to hold 10,000 Union prisoners.
**Casualties:** Over 13,000 Union men died in captivity

*Would that I was an artist & had the material to paint this camp
& all its horors or the tounge of some eloquent Statesman and
had the privleage of expresing my mind to our hon. rulers at
Washington, I should gloery to describe this hell on earth where
it takes 7 of its ocupiants to make a shadow. (sic)*
—Sgt. David Kennedy, 9th Ohio Cavalry, diary entry

"Hell on earth" is where prisoners at Andersonville, or Fort Sumter
as it was called when it was built, found themselves if they were
among the 45,000 Union soldiers forced to call this camp home at
one point during the prison's 14 months of operation at the time of
the American Civil War. Andersonville still haunts the names and
reputations of soldiers from both sides of the war, and the thousands
who perished here under the harshest of conditions are said to still
roam the grounds.

Up until the summer of 1863, the Union and Confederate armies had prisoner exchange agreements, but when this bit of goodwill ended, the amount of captives rose quickly—each side needed a place to hold prisoners of war. But neither side was well equipped to hold thousands of men.

*"Andersonville Prison as seen by John L. Ransom"*
*Image courtesy of the Library of Congress*

It was in November 1863 that the site of this now infamous prison was picked. Confederate forces needed a stockade to hold their captives, and General W. Sidney Winder thought he found the perfect location in a village in south central Georgia. Andersonville had a population of only 20 people at the time, so the political backlash of housing a major military prison would be insignificant. The site wasn't far from the Southwestern Railroad, so moving prisoners and supplies wouldn't be a problem, and the location was deep enough south that if the front lines ever came within sight of it, the Southern cause was lost already.

General Winder's second cousin, Capt. Richard B. Winder, arrived in late December of 1863 and selected a patch of land that was roughly 16.5 acres and had a stream running through the middle of it. The idea was that the men could get fresh water from the highest point in the stream, could bathe in the middle ground, and could use the lowest section of the stream as a latrine. By building canal-like locks on both ends of the stream at the stockade, the prison could flush the stream with fresh water once a day. This was the idea, but the lock system was never built.

On August 9, 1864, after one particularly stormy and rainy period, the Andersonville prisoners did catch what they believed to be a supernatural break. The heavy summer rain swelled the ground, and a natural spring burst forth from the ground, offering the men a fresh water supply. They named it Providence Spring because they felt the gift was truly divine. Today a monument stands where the spring was, and inside is a bowl purchased by former Andersonville prisoners to commemorate the occurrence that saved many lives.

By pressing local slaves into a labor force, Capt. Richard Winder constructed a stockade 1,010 feet long and 780 feet wide made from the pine trees in the region. About 20 feet inside the perimeter they built a light fence, with the ominous name "deadline." If a prisoner crossed the deadline to approach the stockade, he would be shot (or "paroled," as one Union diary entry put it—it seems gallows humor wasn't lost on the prisoners) on sight by the sentries. Upon completion, the site was given the name Fort Sumter but later renamed to Andersonville to distinguish it from the historic Fort Sumter in Charleston Harbor, South Carolina— the site where the first shots of the American Civil War were fired.

By February, when the prison was complete, Capt. Winder felt it could hold 10,000 prisoners, and the facility was turned over to Captain Henry Wirz according to the command of Gen. Winder. Wirz would serve as commandant of the prison where he tried to manage the overwhelming needs of his men and the prison population. Circumstances would soon push the prisoner capacity well beyond 10,000 and significantly further than what would be considered humane.

By June, there were 20,000 men inside the stockade fences of Andersonville Prison, and by the middle of the month, the Confederates were forced to expand by 10 more acres. The northern walls were extended 610 feet and were constructed by able-bodied prisoners and slaves. By August, there were more than 33,000 Union prisoners living—and dying—on the 26.5-acre prison. Captain Wirz sent letters pleading for more resources and supplies, but the struggling Confederacy couldn't offer much of anything.

There were some escapes from Andersonville. Some prisoners took a simple, yet innovative way of getting out. Some played possum, as we learn from reading the May 16, 1864, diary entry of prisoner John Ransom, a Sergeant in the 9th Michigan Cavalry:

> *A funny way of escape has just been discovered by Wirz. A man pretends to be dead and is carried out on a stretcher and left with a row of dead. As soon as it gets dark, Mr. Dead-man jumps up and runs. Wirz, suspecting the trick, took to watching and discovered a "dead man" running away. An examination now takes place by the surgeon before being permitted out from under guard. I hear a number have gotten away by this method, and it seems very probable, as dead men are so plenty that not much attention is paid to them.*

The lucky escaped. Those who lived within the stockades of this prison wasted away. Years later, during the 1865 war crimes trial of Captain Wirz, Dr. John C. Bates testified regarding the conditions inside the prison. Dr. Bates was a Confederate doctor assigned to Andersonville Prison on September 19, 1864, and reported for duty three days later. He worked there until March 29, 1865. During has testimony, he said:

> *Upon going to the hospital I went immediately to the ward to which I was assigned, and, although I am not an over-sensitive man, I must confess I was rather shocked at the appearance of things. The men were lying partially nude and dying, and lousy, a portion of them in the sand and others upon boards which had been stuck up on little props, pretty well crowded together, a majority of them in small tents that were not very serviceable at best. I went around and examined all that were placed in my charge. That was the condition of the men . . . the men would gather around me and ask me for a bone. I would grant their requests so far as I saw bones. I would give them whatever I could find at my disposition without robbing others. I knew well that an appropriation of one ration took it from the general issue; that when I appropriated an extra ration to one man, some one else would fall minus upon that ration. I then fell back upon the distribution of bones . . ..*

*Union prisoners became walking skeletons from malnourishment and disease. Thirteen thousand prisoners lost their lives to the conditions at Andersonville Prison. Photos courtesy of the National Archives*

Dr. Bates went on to describe the infestation of lice among the prisoners, the extreme starvation that turned men into skeletons and then corpses, and the abject squalor of tattered tents made from scraps of cloth and blankets that provided hardly any cover from the elements. Men turned into animals—pouncing on those who died (or were in their final hours, anyway) for the little clothing or food they had.

During the summer of 1865, Union General Sherman was making great progress in driving through Georgia. The Union was closing in, and the prisoner population of Andersonville fell to about 5,000. Once Atlanta was captured by Gen. Sherman, the South knew they were in their final days of rebellion.

By the end of the war, Captain Henry Wirz was charged with war crimes for the abuse and torture of Union prisoners and was hung for it. In Capt. Wirz's defense, one needs to remember that the prisoners were receiving the same rations as their Confederate guards. Food and supplies were scarce for the Confederacy, and given the choice between feeding your own men and feeding your prisoners, well, that wasn't much of a choice at all. The Andersonville prisoners weren't intentionally abused, but they were overcrowded beyond belief. The entire region lacked the provisions needed for that many human beings to survive, and thousands died as a result.

Part of Andersonville's post-war reputation downfall was their thorough record-keeping. Of the 13,000 men who died, only 460 were unknown. Most other prisons on both sides of the war didn't keep any records at all other than general inmate numbers. At Andersonville, they had a name—mostly because a Union prisoner named Dorence Atwater was ordered by his captors to keep records of the men who died here. When the war was winding down, Atwater made a duplicate copy of his records so there would be an account of those who had lost their lives. Atwater published his list when the war ended so the families of the fallen would know what became of their kin.

"Numbers are cold," said Kevin Frye, an Andersonville Prison historian, researcher, and a volunteer at the site today. "But when you see individual names, and those names mean mothers, fathers, brothers, sisters, family— it brings the reality that each individual name that you see was a person."

After the war, the North needed a target to focus the Union's anger on, and the commandant of the facility was simply the logical choice. Captain Henry Wirz didn't stand a chance once the war was over. He was the only Confederate soldier convicted and executed for war crimes during the Civil War.

Kevin Frye has lived near Andersonville Prison since the late 1980s, and he provides a service where he offers to look up prisoner names and also take grave marker photos for those who don't live close enough to visit. "I don't believe nor do I disbelieve as far as the ghosts in Andersonville, though I will say that I've been allowed to stay in the park by myself at night and I've been in both the stockade at midnight as well as the cemetery at midnight, and it's a totally different feeling."

"How so?" I asked.

"In the stockade, the only way I can really describe it is that it's an unsettling feeling," he said. "I really can't put any other words to it besides that. I really take the history seriously and to think that I'm walking on the same grounds that these men did. I think it's more of an aura that I feel.

"The few strange experiences that I've had basically involve my digital camera not working. Even now, a lot of times when I'm in the

*November 10, 1865—Captain Wirz is read his death warrant*
*in Washington, D.C. Photo courtesy of the Library of Congress*

cemetery as well as the stockade taking pictures for folks, sometimes my camera just will not work. I feel like an idiot because, although I don't believe and I don't disbelieve, I'll say out loud, 'I just wanna take a couple, now.' And then the camera works fine. It's really odd."

There are several predominant legends surrounding the ghosts of Andersonville Prison. Along the cemetery wall where Highway 49 curves by, passers-by have reported seeing a male figure standing by the road during rainstorms. The spirit of Father Peter Whelan, a Catholic priest who was a Confederate chaplain from Savannah, Georgia, has been seen around the stockade. Father Whelan was one of the few figures here who was honestly liked by both his comrades and the Union prisoners. Capt. Wirz has also been seen near the stockade—still watching over his final charge.

Inside the stockade there have been other sightings, some kind of non-descript while others have been very specific.

Frye recalls being contacted by a tourist who felt she had made a connection while walking through the prison grounds. "She said that her husband was in the museum, and she had walked out into the center of the stockade area at the top of the hill where it dives off down to where the creek runs through," Frye said. "She said she was just standing there with her eyes closed trying to absorb everything, and in her head she heard a voice say something. She looked around, but there wasn't anybody around. She thought, 'Were you a prisoner here?' And she said a voice came back and said, 'Yes.' Then she said, 'Did you die here?' And the voice said, 'Yes.' She opened her eyes up and she spoke and said, 'What was your name?' The name was given to her. Unfortunately, I've lost all that because of a computer crash, but she told me after she got the name the museum was closing and she didn't have time to research anything, and she said, 'Can you check and see if this guy was here?' It wasn't your typical 'John Smith.' It was a bizarre name. I pulled it up in the computer and yes, the guy was there and did die here."

Harold "Pappy" Harmon, a Civil War reenactor with the 28th Georgia and 123rd New York Volunteer Infantry, visited Andersonville on the weekend of March 10–11, 2001, with his organization. "If you go out on the actual prison ground itself within the marked area, and you can do this at high noon, and you can stand there and look around and be told what happened there and not feel something, then you're not very human," Harmon said.

"Did you experience anything unexplained while you were there?" I asked.

"You feel a coldness," he said. "You'll be standing there and it'll be just like you walked into a freezer. Your bones will hurt from the cold, but yet you could take three or four steps to the left or right and it will be warm like it was to begin with. Or you'll be standing there and you feel a breeze but there's no breeze blowing anywhere. Or you'll hear noises.

"At Andersonville we went out haint huntin' one night. We went to the creek down there and we crossed over the creek, and we were walking along the bottom land there. We got up on the road and the lady with us turned and said, 'Hey, did you see him?' And I said, 'Did I see who?' She said there was a guy walking with us back there. Well, there wasn't anybody back there. It was just me and her."

Pappy Harmon's group had a second experience at Andersonville. While camped at the site for a living history program, some members of his group made their way to the site of Providence Spring at night. While standing at the spring, they noticed a fog start to appear at the far end of the stockade grounds. They walked toward it, the temperature dropped, and they said the fog swirled around them. They noticed dark forms within the fog that they soon discovered were tree trunks or bushes, and further up the hill they noticed several other dark forms. As they climbed the hill, they suddenly found themselves out of the fog. When they turned around, the layer of fog had completely vanished, and the only object on the hill that could account for one of the dark forms was a corner marker. They will never know what the other dark forms in the icy fog could have been.

# 18

# FORT ZACHARY TAYLOR

**War:** United States Civil War (1861–1865)
**Year built:** Construction began in 1845 and the fort
was completed in 1861
**Date of battles:** No battles were fought here; however, the base
has never left Federal hands since it was built
**Location:** Key West, Florida
**Participants:** Union Captain John Brannan and his artillery command
**Casualties:** About 400 between 1860 and 1910

No battles were ever fought at Fort Zachary Taylor in Key West, Florida, but, had the base never been built, the entire Gulf Coast of the United States would have been susceptible to naval attack or invasion. Fort Taylor was built as part of the United States' Third System of fortifications and placed a stronghold in a previously weak area. Though no shots were fired at or from this fort, more than 400 soldiers died during a 50-year period, mainly from yellow fever and other similar diseases. According to many accounts, some of these soldiers have hung around long past their tours have ended. Whether they feel bound by duty, or simply don't know the fort is secure, we can only speculate, but we do know that many people are sighting the ghosts of U.S. Civil War–era soldiers.

Once the Revolutionary War had ended in 1783, the United States set out constructing defense systems along its borders. After the War of 1812, when America was invaded by the British, this need for defense became even more evident—the young nation was prone. Florida became a state in 1845, that same year the U.S. Congress passed a $3 million appropriation to build forts along the Florida reef system to protect this new state and its plethora of coastline. From this funding, Fort Zachary Taylor, named in honor of the 12th U.S. president, was born.

Construction was arduous—labor and building materials needed to come in by boat from the mainland, and the elements didn't always cooperate. A year after construction began, a hurricane plowed through the Keys killing four of the workers. In later years, a lack of the promised funding also paused construction as did more hurricanes and a yellow fever outbreak. Over the years, construction on the three-tiered, trapezoidal fort plodded along, and it wasn't until the end of 1860 that the fort was ready for occupancy. But by this time another storm was brewing—the United States Civil War.

In December 1860, U.S. Artillery Captain John Brannan wrote to Washington, D.C., and asked for instructions on what to do if Florida secedes from the Union. By mid-January, a reply came informing him to move his men into the fort and hold the position—the Union was not going to walk away from this outpost as they had from some others. On January 15, 1861, Capt. Brannan, 44 of his men, and 16 civilian workers marched in and locked Fort Taylor down. Sixty cannons were ready to defend the fort and they had supplies for four months. Fort Taylor never left Federal hands throughout the Civil War—considering its position in the Florida Keys, the fort also wasn't an advantageous target for the Confederacy because taking the fort would have been costly, and the real fight was to the north.

During the mid-1880s, Secretary of War William Endicott and his "Endicott Board" ordered Fort Taylor's top two tiers removed, and the coastal artillery was to be upgraded. Many cannons and artifacts were buried in the casements during the refitting. When World War II became a reality for America in the 1940s, the artillery was upgraded again—this time to anti-aircraft turrets. In 1947, the fort's military tour of duty ended and the site was given to the Navy, who used it to store scrap, and then it was turned over to the state of Florida in 1976 where it evolved into a living museum.

Harry Smid is a 53-year-old man who has worked for the Florida Park Service since the late 1990s. The Park Service manages Fort Taylor today. Smid is also a Civil War reenactor and has given many tours of Fort Taylor as part of his duties there. He was drawn into the fort by the history and said he hadn't heard anything about the ghosts until he started working there and came across a newspaper article from the late 1960s.

In 1968, Howard England, an architect for the Navy, was assigned to investigate and furnish a report on the overgrown dumpsite known as Fort Taylor. England's discovery of so many Civil War artifacts started his passion for uncovering more and learning what secrets to the past the grounds held. "In 1968, this guy, Howard England, was doing excavations of the fort, and he uncovered a variety of cannon, cannon-balls, and all kinds of artifacts," Smid said. "He's doing his excavating and such down in the casement and he takes a break. He feels a presence in the room with him, he turns around, and there's this soldier—clear as day—standing there, and the soldier asks Mr. England, 'What be ya looking for, sonny?' And England tells him that he's looking for a cannon. Well, the spirit introduces himself as this guy by the name of Wendell Gardener, and he tells England all you have to do is dig over this way and you'll find all kinds of stuff. Later, when England continues with his excavations essentially where the ghost suggested that he should dig, he uncovers tons of cannon and cannonballs. That's the first recordings of [the ghosts] that we're aware of. There may have been sightings much earlier, I don't know.

"When this story hit the press in 1968 about the discovery of all these artifacts and how they were discovered, about six weeks later Mr. England gets a visit from these folks from Massachusetts. They wanted to thank him for finally figuring out what in the world happened to their long-lost rela-tive, Wendell Gardner, who happened to be a sergeant in the artillery here."

"What about the staff who works there today? Are they experiencing the ghosts, too?" I asked.

"From time to time we've seen some spirits there," Smid said. "I'm not the only one who's seen them. Just about the entire staff has seen spirits at one time or another.

"One of our former rangers was closing one night. Our park is a day-use park, and one of the things that we do when we're closing up is to make sure that no one is left inside. This ranger hears this ruckus going on in there, and he turns around and he sees this guy standing up on one of the batteries—where they're not supposed to be. The ranger yells, 'Hey!' and the spirit comes running down and stops about 20 feet in front of him. The spirit's dressed in a Civil War uniform. They look at each other, and the spirit turns around and goes through the wall, and the ranger says, 'I'm outta here. I've had enough of this noise. [*laughs*]

"When I first started working here and I was doing the closure procedures at nighttime, I drove through the fort on the parade grounds in my golf cart and I see these shadows inside the mess halls. We're always concerned that there are people who are breaking into the place and trying to steal artifacts and whatnot, so I'd stop, but I didn't see anything. I'd see the shadows moving and then I wouldn't see anything—I thought, Well, this is kind of odd. It was about four years ago when I first started seeing the stuff, and then all of a sudden it kind of dawned on me that maybe that's what I'm seeing."

"That you're seeing ghosts?" I asked.

"Right," Smid said. "Last year a couple of us decided to do some actual ghost hunting in there. Key West is known for being a haunted place. There's a lot of spirits all over the place, and our community service organization, the Friends of Fort Taylor, was considering doing ghost tours. So we had these folks come in with their scientific instruments and whatnot, and they're doing all these readings. It was a moonless night, a clear night, and we're inside the fort. I'm on the parade ground with one of the ghost hunters there, and we're seeing the shadows darting back and forth between the mess halls and I'm thinking, okay, this is really clear—clear as day that I'm seeing this stuff. I'm not getting freaked out or anything but this is odd.

"I see some activity going on inside the sally port as we walk by, and I know that there's no one else in there. There were six of us, and two of us were on the parade ground and the other four had gone up on top of one of the other batteries. So I see this action going on inside the sally port, and I ask my partner, 'Should I call out to it?' And she says, 'Why not.' So I come to attention and yell out, 'Sergeant. Post!' And the spirit stops. It stops walking and turns toward me. I can't make out anything for sure except it's some sort of a shadow. I yell, 'Post!' and it stops. It takes a step forward, and I think, Oh shit, I don't know what I've gotten myself into here. I kinda freaked out, I guess. I said, 'The fort is secure. Carry on.' And the shadow about-faces and goes away."

"Post" is a command one yells to a guard on duty to get his attention. It turns out that this first face-to-face encounter wasn't Smid's last, either. In 2005, Fort Taylor had a Halloween event inside where they set up a haunted spook house with props, mazes, and other obligatory fun house items. Smid was stationed inside for the event. "I'm in my Civil War uniform, and I'm there in the casement where we are paying homage to all of those who died at the fort. There were six big chalkboards set up with all of the names—the 400-plus names written on them. The casement is lit with a lantern, so I'm waiting for a group to come by and out of the corner of my eye I noticed something. I turned and I see a soldier come walking in to the casement. He sits down on the cistern well and just sits there checking stuff out. This is about 10 feet away from me and I'm thinking, Oh my God, what is going on here? I wanted to go over, but couldn't muster the courage to go over and talk to it. This all happened in the span of about 30 seconds, but it seemed like minutes and minutes. So I finally go over and attempt to see what's going on, and the spirit just kind of dissipates."

Smid wasn't the only person to experience the supernatural during their Halloween festivities. He mentioned another volunteer that was working near the latrine area of the fort, who said that at one point a number of phantom soldiers came in to use the latrine. The volunteer was shaken by what he'd seen—it's not often one catches a ghost relieving himself.

# *Part X*

Black Hills War

(1876–1877)

# 19

# LITTLE BIGHORN

**War:** Black Hills War (1876–1877)
**Dates of battle:** June 25–26, 1876
**Location:** Little Bighorn River, Big Horn County, Montana
**Participants:** About 6,000–7,000 Native Americans made up of
Sioux, Lakota, Northern Cheyenne, and Arapaho under Sitting Bull and
Crazy Horse against roughly 650 American troops under Lt. Col. George
Armstrong Custer
**Casualties:** About 350 killed

On November 9, 1875, Indian Inspector E. C. Watkins issued a report that
said many Lakota and Northern Cheyenne Indians were openly hostile
to the United States. These "hostiles" also happened to live in the
gold-rich Black Hills in the region that would soon become Montana.
To answer this potential crisis, the 7th Cavalry under Lt. Col. George A.
Custer were called in. Thirty-one officers, 566 troopers, 30–40 scouts,
and a few civilians comprised the 7th as they made their way north from
Fort Riley, Kansas, toward the Black Hills in the spring of 1876. Many
were marching to their doom, and Custer was heading for his last stand.

*Lt. Col. George A. Custer,*
*Photo courtesy of the Library*
*of Congress*

On June 15, the 7th Cavalry picked up a large trail—their Indian foes were recently on the move. During a night march on June 24–25, some of Custer's scouts reported that a large encampment of Indians was nearby. Custer divided his force into four detachments, the largest consisting of 13 officers and 198 men that Custer would personally lead. Custer's detachment marched the ridge on the eastern bank of the Little Bighorn River with the objective of attacking the camp from the north. The other three detachments were ordered to scout the region outside of the camp, engage any Indians they found, and also stand by in case reinforcements were needed.

The American's 7th Cavalry didn't know what force lay inside the encampment waiting for them, and this lack of military intelligence would soon prove costly. As the initial American attack closed in, they discovered Lakota and Northern Cheyenne en masse and ready to fight—none had the notion of running away. As shots began to ring out, Custer's detachment soon realized they were outnumbered by almost five to one. They didn't last very long.

George Herendon, a scout with the 7th Cavalry, relayed what he witnessed at the Little Bighorn battle to a *New York Herald* reporter in July 1876. "We stayed in the bush about three hours, and I could hear heavy firing below in the river, apparently about 2 miles distant. I did not know who it was, but knew the Indians were fighting some of our men, and learned afterward it was Custer's command. Nearly all the Indians in the upper part of the valley drew off down the river, and the fight with Custer lasted about one hour, when the heavy firing ceased."

In the aftermath, 263 of the 7th Cavalrymen lay dead including George Custer. Estimates put the Native American dead between 60 and 100. The Indians won the battle, but simply lacked the military might and numbers to win the war. Both sides were fighting for their way of life, their country, and their home. The passion of these soldiers has left a permanent mark on the valley around the Little Bighorn River.

Ghosts of both United States and Indian warriors have been heard and seen in several areas of the monument grounds that stand here today. As with many other battlefields, some have witnessed pieces of the battle replaying itself, and others have heard screams of men in mortal peril. One former park ranger who is also a Crow Indian once witnessed two Indians holding shields on horseback up the bluff from the river. She said she felt no danger, but did sense that they were either Sioux or Cheyenne spirits.

General Custer has been said to roam the area around the Visitor's Center late at night, possibly making one last inspection. Another unidentified United States soldier dressed in a brown shirt has also been seen in the Visitor's Center.

The monuments and battlefield of Little Bighorn stand as a solemn reminder of what took place here in 1876. For the United States, the Black Hills War was about conquering land, ensuring its way of life, and pushing potentially hostile peoples away. For the Indians, the war was about defending their homeland against a foreign invader with a stronger military. The ghosts who still wander here serve as a reminder that some wars have no winner.

# Part XI

World War I

(1914–1918)

# 20

# THE BOWMEN OF MONS

**War:** World War I (1914–1918)
**Date of battle:** August 23, 1914
**Location:** Mons, Belgium
**Participants:** 70,000 British Expeditionary Force (BEF) troops under Commander-in-Chief Sir John French against 160,000 German troops under General Alexander von Kluck
**Casualties:** Over 6,600

> . . . the men all chilled to the bone, almost too exhausted to move and with the depressing consciousness of defeat weighing heavily upon them. A bad defeat, there can be no gain saying it . . . we had been badly beaten, and by the English—by the English we had so laughed at a few hours before.
>
> —Walter Bloem, Reserve Captain,
> 12th Brandenburg Grenadier Regiment

Mons was the first battle of World War I between the British and the Germans. In August 1914, British forces crossed the English Channel and landed in France with the task of augmenting French General Lanrezac's Fifth Army and pushing the German army back through Belgium and home to Germany. After the initial landing, 70,000 British Expeditionary Force (BEF) troops were cautiously making their way into Belgium from the coast when they encountered German cavalry patrols on August 22. The British Commander-in-Chief, Sir John French, made the snap decision to engage his enemy immediately against the counsel of his intelligence officers who wanted to wait until they could combine forces with France before attacking the Germans. But Sir John French insisted, and his gross underestimation of the size of the German forces led to a massive battle the following day, which then led to a supernatural tale that has yet to completely die even though the creator of that tale has disputed the story in writing.

After spotting the German cavalry units, Sir John French ordered his units to take up defensive positions at the Mons Canal. German General von Kluck wanted to outflank the British Expeditionary Force (BEF), surround them entirely, and finish them off, but the German High Command didn't want von Kluck to be cut off from other German forces because if the plan backfired, it would be von Kluck's forces who were wiped out. Early in the morning of August 23, von Kluck opted for a full frontal attack against the British position at Mons. Numbers and guns were in the Germans' favor, and they intended to make the confrontation a costly one for the British.

After the opening salvo of artillery, the Germans advanced, but they were gunned down by the hundreds. The British riflemen were deadly accurate, so much so that the German commanders thought they were up against a swarm of machine guns. Even with accurate rifles, the British recognized the lopsidedness of the odds. When word came that their French counterparts were in retreat and were not going to join the battle, the BEF began their own retreat to their second line of defense. It's a dangerous endeavor whenever an army turns its back to its enemy, and it is at this point of the battle that the story "The Bowmen" by Arthur Machen started the supernatural legend that is still attached to Mons to this day.

Shortly after reading the newspaper accounts of the battle of Mons, British author Arthur Machen started turning a story over in his head about how the BEF were able to out-kill the Germans and safely retreat. The short story "The Bowmen" first appeared in *The Evening News* in London on September 29, 1914. Below is an excerpt of the story picking up where one of the British soldiers is facing the endless flow of German lines coming for him and his men. At this point, a squad of BEF have resigned themselves to their own doom and can only hope to die with honor, good humor, and take a few Germans out before they go, in hopes that their countrymen further back will have a successful retreat.

*. . . And then he remembered—he says he cannot think why or wherefore—a queer vegetarian restaurant in London where he had once or twice eaten eccentric dishes of cutlets made of lentils and nuts that pretended to be steak. On all the plates in this restaurant there was printed a figure of St. George in blue, with the motto, Adsit Anglis Sanctus Georgius—May St. George be a present help to the English. This soldier happened to know Latin and other useless things, and now, as he fired at his man in the grey advancing mass—300 yards away—he uttered the pious motto. He went on firing to the end, and at last Bill on his right had to clout him cheerfully over the head to make him stop, pointing out as he did so that the King's ammunition cost money and was not lightly to be wasted in drilling funny patterns into dead Germans.*

*For as the Latin scholar uttered his invocation he felt something between a shudder and an electric shock pass through his body The roar of the battle died down in his ears to a gentle murmur; instead of it, he says, he heard a great voice and a shout louder than a thunder—peal crying, "Array, array, array!"*

*His heart grew hot as a burning coal, it grew cold as ice within him, as it seemed to him that a tumult of voices answered to his summons. He heard or seemed to hear, thousands shouting:*

*St. George! St. George!*

*Ha! Messier; ha! Sweet Saint, grant us good deliverance!*

*St. George for merry England!*

*Harrow! Harrow! Monseigneur St. George, succour us.*

*Ha! St. George! Ha! St. George! A long bow and a strong bow. Heaven's Knight, aid us!*

*And as the soldier heard these voices he saw before him, beyond the trench, a long line of shapes, with a shining about them. They were like men who drew the bow, and with another shout, their cloud of arrows flew singing and tingling through the air towards the German hosts.*

The story goes on to describe the Germans falling by the thousands at the hands of St. George and his Agincourt Bowmen who had descended from Heaven to hold the line while the British retreated. The story describes the air as being dark with a flood of singing arrows that found their marks in the German army.

When the real battle of Mons had ended, an estimated 1,600 British troops were dead compared to more than 5,000 German. The battle was seen as a British victory not only because they stood against overwhelming odds, but because they outgunned their enemy so effectively. When news of the battle hit the British newspapers, military recruitment numbers leaped as young British men were eager to join the fight. Arthur Machen's fictionalized account of the divine intervention that took place there made Mons's legend grow to epic proportions.

In the 1915 book called *The Bowmen and Other Legends of the War*, Machen republished his "Angels of Mons" short story with a lengthy introduction regarding the events of the previous 10 months since the story was first published. In the introduction, Machen speculated as to how his supernatural account grew:

> . . . *in a few days from its publication the editor of The Occult Review wrote to me. He wanted to know whether the story had any foundation in fact. I told him that it had no foundation in fact of any kind or sort; I forget whether I added that it had no foundation in rumor, but I should think not, since to the best of my belief there were no rumors of heavenly interposition in existence at that time. Certainly I had heard of none. Soon afterwards the editor of Light wrote asking a like question, and I made him a like reply. It seemed to me that I had stifled any "Bowmen" mythos in the hour of its birth.*
>
> *A month or two later, I received several requests from editors of parish magazines to reprint the story. I—or, rather, my editor—readily gave permission; and then, after another month or two, the conductor of one of these magazines wrote to me, saying that the February issue containing the story had been sold out, while there was still great demand for it. Would I allow them to reprint "The Bowmen" as a pamphlet, and would I write a short preface giving the exact authorities for the story? I replied that they might reprint in pamphlet form with all my heart, but that I could not give my authorities, since I had none, the tale being pure invention. The priest wrote again, suggesting—to my amazement—that I must be mistaken, that the main "facts" of "The Bowmen" must be*

*true, that my share in the matter must surely have been confined to the elaboration and decoration of a veridical history. It seemed that my light fiction had been accepted by the congregation of this particular church as the solidest facts; and it was then that it began to dawn on me that if I had failed in the art of letters, I had succeeded unwittingly, in the art of deceit.*

The legend of the angels of Mons grew beyond the pages of a newspaper and the pages of Arthur Machen's book. During almost every war throughout recorded history, people want and need to believe that their cause is just, and so God must be on their side. Machen's Mons angels helped reinforce this idea to the British. The churches propagated the legend, and soon, enough people believed St. George had intervened on the BEF's behalf that even the creator of the tale couldn't squelch the myth.

A great battle was fought at Mons. The odds were overwhelming to the British, yet they prevailed in regard to body count and in stopping German advances that day. As we've seen throughout *Ghosts of War*, where there has been great loss of life in a short period of time, often a haunting will follow. Mons may very well have its ghosts, but its angels are quite another matter. Those religiously inclined may stamp their feet and insist that Machen's Heavenly bowmen were simply a metaphor for what God must have surely done that day in Belgium.

# *Part XII*

World War II

(1939–1945)

# 21

# USS ARIZONA

**War:** World War II (1939–1945)
**Launched:** October 17, 1916, New York Navy Yard
**Class:** Pennsylvania
**Size:** Length: 608 feet; Beam: 106 feet 3 inches
**Draft:** 33 feet 6 inches; Displacement: 31,400 tons
**Service locations:** Eastern seaboard training vessel during World War I. Refitted and modernized in the 1930s and stationed at Pearl Harbor in 1941.
**Crew:** 92 officers, 1,639 enlisted men
**Current location:** Since its sinking on December 7, 1941, the ship has been in Pearl Harbor, Hawaii. A memorial was erected over the site in 1962.
**Casualties:** 1,177

*December 7, 1941—a date which will live in infamy—the United States of America was suddenly and deliberately attacked by naval and air forces of the Empire of Japan.*
            —President Franklin D. Roosevelt, December 8, 1941

The USS *Arizona* (BB–39) never saw combat until its final day afloat. In 1941, the world was at war and the United States was trying its best to stay neutral. The Arizona was part of the Pacific fleet that was keeping a close watch on the waters to the west as diplomatic relations with Japan were steadily breaking down. On December 6, 1941, the *Arizona* moored next to the repair ship *Vestal* (AR–4) in Pearl Harbor. There were 10 other ships in the harbor, all moored close to each other—a configuration that would prove to be catastrophic. Though there have been conspiracy theories as to whether the U.S. government knew the Japanese attack was coming and let the Empire hit the Pacific Fleet on the chin so the American public would support the country's entering World War II, these ideas can be debated. What is certain is that the men on board the *Arizona* certainly did not know of their impending doom at 7:53 AM on December 7 when the attack began. Could more have been done to save the ship if everyone on board were watching the skies that calm, sunny morning? Probably not. But hindsight offers little solace to one ghost who is still seen at the sunken wreck today.

The USS *Arizona* was born under a bad sign. On June 19, 1915, the ship was scheduled to be christened and launched. Certain political forces wanted it christened with water instead of the traditional champagne because the governor of Arizona protested—probably to support the growing contingent of alcohol prohibition supporters in the United States. "Ours is a dry state," said Arizona Governor W. P. Hunt, "with more cows and less milk and more rivers and less water than any other state in the Union. Therefore we naturally favor water." But the old sailors raised their voices against breaking tradition. Luck and superstitions play heavily on the minds of sailors, and they saw no need to tempt fate over something as simple as a christening. "But sailor men are superstitious about a battleship christened with water," Gov. Hunt continued, "so I have decided to compromise, and there will be a bottle of water and a bottle of wine." But the sailor purists didn't like any compromises when it came to the official launch of a ship. On June 19, a bottle of champagne and a bottle of some of the first water to flow through the Hoover Dam was used to christen the *Arizona*.

The *Arizona* didn't see military action during World War I. She sailed for England to join the British Grand Fleet in November of 1918 during the final moments of World War I, but wasn't needed for combat. In the years between wars, she conducted training, went through refittings, and performed fleet exercises. In the 1930s, she was moved to the Pacific and continued her peacetime activities and exercises. As World War II was heating up in the autumn of 1941, the ship headed for the port of Pearl Harbor.

In the early morning hours of December 7, 1941, the Japanese fleet had snuck up on the island of Oahu with 353 planes and five Ko-hyoteki class midget submarines to fire torpedoes at the American ships, which came in two waves. The first wave consisted of torpedo bombers.

The mass of planes was picked up on the Army's Opana Point radar system, but there was confusion because the radar operator was expecting some U.S. B-17 bombers that morning, so no alarm was sounded. The Japanese made it to the heart of the American fleet with almost no confrontation. The American seamen aboard the ships were enjoying a slow Sunday morning when they were awoken by the sounds of explosions. Torpedoes and gunfire rained down from all around as the Japanese squadrons pummeled the sitting American ships. All hands were called to their battle stations, but confusion reined supreme in the critical initial minutes when so many Japanese bombs were finding their targets.

Aboard the USS *Arizona*, an armor-piercing bomb fell from a Japanese bomber and struck the forward ammunition magazine stores, igniting one-and-a-half million pounds of gunpowder that then exploded, tearing off the forward part of the ship and instantly killing any men nearby. The fires burned for two days, and the gasoline and oil in the water around the ship also was aflame—dooming some men who survived the blast but were soon burned up when they dove for the safety of the water.

The cataclysmic damage caused the boat to fill up like a water pail turned on its side in a pond. The more water that rushed in, the faster the ship sank, allowing an even greater intake of ocean water. Within minutes, the *Arizona* was settling on the harbor bottom, taking more than half her crew with her.

An hour and a half after the attack had begun, it was over. The Japanese were disappointed that there were no U.S. aircraft carriers in port that day, but the damage they inflicted was substantial. Overall, 2,403 Americans had perished, 188 American aircraft were destroyed, and 18 ships were sunk including five battleships. The United States of America's neutrality vanished in the span of 90 minutes, and they were now in World War II.

The USS *Arizona* was never raised, nor could it be dismantled underwater or towed away. Initially, the priority for the U.S. Navy was to repair and rebuild the Pacific fleet as quickly as possible. All attention was given to ships that could be repaired or salvaged, and the *Arizona* didn't fall into either of those categories. The Navy received many requests from families of the lost sailors to retrieve the bodies, but those requests were denied. The men who perished were considered buried at sea—buried but not forgotten.

*The USS* Arizona *today.*
*Photo istockphoto.com/John Sfondilias*

I spoke to Richard Senate, an author and lecturer who has been studying ghosts and haunted locations for many years. He first visited the USS *Arizona* in 1987. I asked Senate what drew him to the ship. "My father-in-law was a member of the United States Navy and had served as a petty officer," Senate said. "He was the first one who told me the legend of the ghost officer on the USS *Arizona*. It only happens when the tide is low and part of the ship is exposed that they see an officer. On certain nights, especially at dusk, or in the morning hours, some see an officer saluting the flag. The legend is that he was the officer of the day and for some personal reason, he wasn't at his station. He wasn't where he was supposed to be when the Japanese attack came and he died in the attack. The guilt, because he wasn't at his station, is what causes him to come back and haunt the ship.

"Going over there is a somber experience. I don't know if it is the idea that you are essentially going to a site where the people are still buried, it's a mausoleum under the water, or the fact that you can see the outline of the ship at the modernistic memorial. It has almost a spiritual feeling to the place. Not a feeling of dread. But I would tend to believe that if you are there late at night, it would be far more spooky than it was on a nice, bright, sunny early morning when I first went out there."

Senate went on to describe a second ghost that is said to be seen on the memorial itself. A sailor in dress whites has been spotted walking inside after the site has been closed for the day. The memorial is of course in the harbor, and there is no way to get to it except by boat.

One question I wanted to explore with Richard Senate was an issue I ran into several times while researching this book. A few people, either through e-mail or over the phone, accused me of somehow dishonoring the memories of those who fought and died for their countries by suggesting that these soldiers are ghosts now. "Others have defined the term 'ghost,'" Senate said. "I don't know what ghosts are. They are something that people see and encounter, but others are saying that ghosts are spirits who are cursed, or trapped on another plane, or something like that. But that's not really the case. Ghosts might well be something quite different, and just because someone has said that ghosts are somehow trapped here because of their sins or something like that doesn't make it true.

"I can understand where they're coming from. Maybe they're thinking 'Here's a brave soldier, his soul trapped wandering the earth as a disembodied ghost.' But that's just the definition of 'ghost' that's been forced upon us. It may not be a soul or spirit at all. It could very well be that so many people coming to a place and being emotionally moved might actually project something out there."

# 22

# ARCHERFIELD AIRPORT

**War:** World War II (1939–1945)
**Date of operation:** 1929 to present
**Date of incident:** March 27, 1943
**Location:** Brisbane, Queensland, Australia
**Casualties:** 23

Before 1939, Brisbane's flight needs had to be serviced from a field in the Brisbane suburb of Eagle Farm. The runway often flooded during the wet season, and road and rail access to the strip wasn't convenient, so the search for a new site for the Brisbane aerodrome was underway. In 1927, a QANTAS DeHavilland DH61 piloted by Captain Lester Brain made a successful landing at Franklin's Farm, and he made the recommendation that this site, with its good drainage and access to rail and road, should be the spot for a significant air facility. The airport opened for business on April 1, 1931, but it was during the airport's World War II service that its ghostly legend was born.

When the war broke out in September 1939, the Royal Australian Air Force (RAAF) commandeered some of the hangar space, and, to help build Australia's air force, both the civilian aircraft and the flying instructors were pressed into military service. Construction quickly began on larger hangars to accommodate the influx of airplanes. As the war progressed throughout the South Pacific, Australia became a strategic position for servicing aircrafts, training, and launching sorties.

After the Japanese attack on Pearl Harbor on December 7, 1941, the United States was officially in the war and had to support two fronts—one in Europe and one in the South Pacific. American B17 Bombers (a.k.a. the Flying Fortress), Kittyhawks, and other U.S. air power was moving into Archerfield as was military aircraft from other allied countries. Commercial air traffic was still going in and out of Archerfield as well, which made for an extremely busy skyway, runway, and tarmac. During a particularly wet morning, a Douglas DC3 landed and collided with a Dutch airplane and an American B17, but this wouldn't be the last accident here.

The most significant tragedy happened during an early morning crash of a RAAF C-47 Dakota plane on March 27, 1943. Just after 5 AM the C-47 Dakota, its 36 Squadron RAAF flight crew consisting of the pilot, First Officer Alexander Kenn Arnold; co-pilot, Sgt. Joseph Hammond; fitter, LAC Samuel Ivan Wiles; and wireless operator, Sgt. Lyle Carter Morgan carried their 19 passengers (17 Australian military personnel and two U.S. Army personnel) headed skyward with Sydney as their destination. Just after taking off from Archerfield, the C-47 Dakota pulled into a fog bank and veered southeast. As the plane turned, it lost altitude because the pilot was flying visually (without watching his instruments) and he didn't notice how low to the ground they were. The wing caught a large tree and the plane crashed just outside of the airfield property between Oxley Creek and modern day Bowhill Road. All on board were lost. An investigation into the crash concluded that the cause was pilot error.

A World War II–era pilot—complete with leather jacket, flight cap, and goggles—has been seen wandering the airport grounds and is often sighted on Beatty Road, the street that runs almost parallel to the doomed flightpath of the C-47 Dakota. Some people have said the pilot will smile and wave, others say he just walks along oblivious to the world around him. Could this specter be that of First Officer Alexander Kenn Arnold? Possibly. Archerfield Airport's ghost is now as much a part of the Brisbane landscape and history as the airport he comes from.

# 23

# USS *ALABAMA*

**War:** World War II (1939–1945)
**Launched:** February 16, 1942, Norfolk Navy Yard, Portsmouth, Virginia
**Class:** South Dakota
**Size:** Length: 680 feet; Beam: 108 feet; Draft: 36 feet;
Displacement: 35,000 tons
**Service Locations:** North Atlantic and Pacific Oceans
**Crew:** 127 Officers, 2,205 Enlisted Men
**Current location:** Since 1964, the USS *Alabama* has been permanently
moored at USS *Alabama* Memorial Park, 2703 Battleship Parkway, Mobile,
Alabama. Tel: (251) 433-2703
**Web site:** www.ussalabama.com

The USS *Alabama* (BB–60) was fast. She could make 28 knots with
her 130,000 horsepower engines, and her radar saw farther than most
ships—at least it did when it really counted on June 19, 1944, when
the ship's radar spotted Japanese bombers at an unprecedented 190
miles away. This marked the start of the Battle of the Philippine Sea.
Because the *Alabama* provided so much warning to the surrounding
fleet, when the enemy planes arrived, the U.S. guns were locked,
loaded, and already pointed skyward. In the battle, 400 Japanese
planes were downed.

USS *Alabama*

*Photo by Paul W. Puckett, Jacksonville, Florida*

Though the ship isn't the most famous of the World War II battleships, it is one of the few still preserved. Inside, there may be more than just a floating museum. Ghostly legends surrounding the ship include a blondhaired Ensign who has been spotted in one of the officer's quarters, a phantom turret crew has been reported on the aft deck, and even the cook's galley has its own specter. Many visit the ship today for the role it played in history, and a few also experience the ghosts.

There have been six USS *Alabamas* in the United States Navy. Construction on the first started in 1818. By the time the 74-gun ship was ready to launch in 1864, she was renamed *New Hampshire*—a move that was the result of the United States Civil War. The second *Alabama* was a Cutter that was constructed in 1819; the third was a sidewheel steamer that the Navy acquired in 1849 and served as a troop ship; the fourth (BB-8) was commissioned in 1900 then scrapped in 1924; the fifth (BB-60) is the haunted ship we're discussing here; and the sixth (SSBN-731) is an *Ohio*-class ballistic missile submarine.

The USS *Alabama* (BB-60) was commissioned on August 16, 1942. The United States had officially entered World War II nine months earlier when Pearl Harbor was bombed by the Japanese, and all areas of the United States armed forces were ramping up. When she first entered service, the *South Dakota* class dreadnought battleship was used to augment the British Fleet by escorting convoys of ships on the "Murmansk Run" from England to Russia on the North Sea. The ship was en garde against German vessels that hoped to pick apart supply lines.

Later in her World War II tour of duty, the *Alabama* saw service in the Pacific Ocean. The *'Bama* participated in the attack on Honshu Island, a

Japanese island located 50 miles north of Tokyo. Under the cover of darkness, the ship set her nine 16-inch, 45-caliber guns loose on an engineering factory on the island. Fifteen hundred tons of shells were fired upon mills and factories, and the targets were left in rubble.

After receiving nine battle stars and being credited with downing 22 Japanese planes, the ship was decommissioned in 1947 and sent to Bremerton, Washington, where she awaited her fate. In 1964, enough money was raised to have the ship towed to Mobile, Alabama, where she would become part of the museum there and serve as a reminder of what life and death was like aboard a World War II battleship.

Geri Albea, who now lives in northern Mississippi, recalls her husband telling her about the *Alabama* coming to Mobile. "My husband grew up in Mobile," Albea said. "In grade school he helped collect money to get the USS *Alabama* into Mobile Bay."

Back in October 1985, Albea and her husband went on a sightseeing tour of the USS *Alabama*. She told me about a strange experience she had onboard the ship.

"We were there from 10:30 AM until about three or four in the afternoon," Albea said. "It was a very warm afternoon, and there were only six people touring the ship at the same time. It was three different couples, and we each chose a different route so we would have some privacy. I believe there were three painted lines: red, yellow, and blue at the beginning of the tour, and each route ran through the entire ship but just not together. I wanted to see everything on it and I guess after about 10 minutes into the tour I just had this feeling that something or someone was watching me, and it was just an uncanny feeling. I kept turning around but there was never anyone else anywhere near us."

"In what part of the ship were you getting these strange feelings?" I asked.

"We had completed the kitchen tour and were going up some stairs up to another level. The feeling was real strong in the hospital ward— I guess what they called the 'sick bay'—and my husband, he wouldn't have any part of it. But I was so obvious with turning around—I never said anything to him, but I did keep looking over my shoulder and he said, 'What is going on? Why are you doing that?' I said, 'I just feel like something is watching me.' And from that time on, he made fun of me.

"When we finished our tour, we were coming back out and there was this lieutenant's quarters—it was just a small bunk area, and I went in and sat down on the little bunk for just a second. It was like there was an aura around me or something, it was like a presence. When I got up to come back out, something snatched my diamond earring out of my ear. Had it just fallen out, I wouldn't have noticed it, but my hair moved and there was a tug or something on my ear. I'm a real fanatic about my jewelry, and I thought 'Ohhh my husband's going to fuss about this because he's going to have to replace it.' When we found the earring, it was over in a corner, probably 10 to 12 feet from where I felt the snatch at . . . and the back was still on my earring when I found it."

"Was your ear torn?" I asked.

"No."

"So it's kind of impossible that the back would be on your earring," I said.

"Right. That ended it for me. I wasn't spooked or scared of the ship or anything. It's just that I knew I had not been imagining all of the feelings that I had when I was on the ship. I guess you have to be a female to understand that when you have an earring with the back clipped on it, when the earring drops out, you're not going to find the earring with the back still on."

There is a bond that Navy crewmen have with their ship and with each other. There's a reason so many captains went down with their ships in battle. It's a code of duty and honor to serve their country and protect their ship at all costs. Sometimes even death can't break that bond.

# 24

# BIGGIN HILL

**War:** World War II (1939–1945)
**Dates of operation:** 1918 to present
**Location:** London, England

*. . . I have slipped the surly bonds of Earth And danced the skies on laughter-silvered wings; Sunward I've climbed, and joined the tumbling mirth Of sun-split clouds,—and done a hundred things. . .*

—John Gillespie Magee Jr.,
Spitfire pilot, September 1941

One question that occasionally comes up when discussing ghosts sounds a bit funny at first, but it's actually a very legitimate question: Why aren't spirits naked? After all, maybe a person has a soul or spirit inside, but his pants, shirt, and coat certainly cannot. We can only theorize as to why this is. First, maybe the disembodied spirit is projecting exactly how they want to look—the age they want to appear, the dress, and even the emotion on their faces. Or it's possible that ghosts are impressions left on the land—some event that was somehow recorded into the very fabric of space and time, and some living people are able to tune into this phenomenon. In this case, there are no spirits or souls, just a playback of a long-ago event. In the area of Biggin Hill in the southeastern London borough of Bromley, a ghost has been seen in the skies above. But this ghost isn't a man: it's a World War II Royal Air Force Spitfire airplane.

In 1918, an aerodrome was constructed on the high ground of Biggin Hill. The Royal Air Force knew this would be a defensive position to protect London. Biggin Hill also boasts two firsts: the first aircraft to conduct air-to-ground communications flew out of this site, as did the first British airplane to shoot down a German aircraft in the Second World War.

In some cases, witnesses have reported hearing the old Spitfire coming in for a landing. Others have claimed to see the airplane flying low to the ground briefly before it vanishes. The legend says that a Royal Air Force airman crashed his plane over the ridge in the tiny nearby town of Tatsfield and it is his plane that can be heard. Some legends also suggest the pilot's ghost has been seen in full World War II-era flight gear walking back to Biggin Hill airport.

# RMS QUEEN MARY

**War:** World War II (1939–1945)
**Launched:** September 16, 1934, Clydebank, Scotland
**Size:** Length: 1,019.5 feet; Beam: 118.5 feet; Displacement: 77,400 tons
**Service locations:** North Atlantic and Pacific Oceans
**Crew:** 1,101 crew; 2,139 passengers
**Current location:** Since 1967, the RMS *Queen Mary* has been
permanently moored at 1126 Queens Highway, Long Beach, California.

RMS Queen Mary: *a noble tribute to the imagination of man.*
—H. M. Tomlinson

The RMS *Queen Mary* was built as a transatlantic ocean liner by the
Cunard White Star Line. Why would a cruise ship be in a book about
the ghosts of war? This is no ordinary ship—the *Queen Mary* was one
of several passenger liners pressed into military service during World
War II. She was painted with gray paint to help conceal her from
enemy planes and boats and was given the ominous nickname "The
Grey Ghost." Built to hold about 3,200 passengers and crew comfortably,
she sometimes ferried over 15,000 servicemen across the Atlantic and
even into the Indian Ocean—a move that would prove deadly. Today
the *Queen Mary* is a permanently moored floating hotel in Long
Beach, California, but she's also one of the most haunted places in
the world.

*The RMS* Queen Mary.
*istockphoto.com/Rodolfo Arpia*

The *Queen Mary* was a hot target for German U-boats and bombers. Adolf Hitler offered large cash rewards and the Iron Cross medal to any U-boat commander who could sink her. Because she often had little or no military escort when crossing the ocean, the ship ran in a zigzag pattern with orders to never stop until port in order to avoid becoming an easy torpedo target. During one such run on October 2, 1942, the *Queen Mary* was being escorted by the HMS *Curacoa*, a World War I–era light cruiser. The *Curacoa* crossed in front of the *Queen Mary* and was practically sliced in half by the giant cruise liner. All 338 British sailors perished when the *Curacoa* quickly sank to the bottom.

During one overladen voyage, the *Queen Mary* was carrying more than 15,000 troops across the Indian Ocean in sweltering heat. The ship was meant to be a North Atlantic liner so there was little that could be done to circulate cooler air throughout the decks of the ship. Dozens of men died from suffocation or heat exposure because the conditions were so difficult.

After World War II, the *Queen Mary* returned to her civilian service, but transatlantic ocean liner travel was becoming a thing of the past. Airplanes were becoming the way to cross the ocean post-war, and vacation cruises took place in the warmer climes of the Caribbean and through the Panama Canal. The *Queen Mary* was too big for the Canal, and she wasn't made for the heat—something she'd already proved. On December 11, 1967, she made her final docking in Long Beach, California, where she became permanently moored and now serves as a hotel and banquet facility.

With so much death in and around "The Grey Ghost," there seems to be some residual hauntings left over today. Psychic medium Peter James, who was the resident psychic on the television show *Sightings*, has been investigating the ghosts of the *Queen Mary* since 1991. He's conducted many tours of the ship, spent countless overnights there, and believes there are at least 600 active resident ghosts. When asked about the *Curacoa* collision, James said, "To this day, you can hear the collision—the residual sound effects and also the water splashing and many screams for help."

Other ghostly reports aboard this ship include phantom smells such as cigar smoke, which Tony Mellard, a California resident, once experienced while on one of Peter James's ghost tours on the *Queen Mary*. The Winston Churchill suite is said to be among the most haunted on the ship, and smelling phantom cigar smoke is often a prelude to something more significant. "That night, my wife and I started exploring the hallways of the ship," Mellard said. "We walked into the strongest smell of cigar smoke you could imagine. It just seemed to come out of nowhere, and it was literally as if someone were standing right in front of us blowing smoke right in our faces— yet we could see no visible smoke. The oddest thing about it was that the smell seemed to linger in one certain area in the middle of the hallway, and if you took one step away in any direction, it would disappear. And as soon as you stepped back, *bam*, it would overcome your sense of smell. In all our excitement, we really weren't paying attention to where we were on the ship. But in the midst of our chattering, my wife looks over at the wall and says, 'Oh my God, look!' There was the big, golden plaque on the door—'Sir Winston Churchill Suite.' It sent chills up our spines."

Mellard has also heard voices on board. Could they be the voices of those who died aboard the *Curacoa* or perhaps those who perished in the sweltering heat? "I have heard the voices," he said. "They seem to almost reverberate out of the ship itself—almost like a clanging of metal that forms itself into words. It's really bizarre."

# 26

# COSFORD ROYAL AIR FORCE BASE

**War:** World War II (1939–1945)
**Dates of operation:** 1938 to present
**Location:** Shropshire, England

Cosford Royal Air Force Base opened its doors in 1938 as a place to maintain and store aircraft and to train the men and women who would assemble, repair, and service the planes for the British military. Hundreds of thousands of people have passed through the base's programs before moving forward in their RAF careers. Though some of these technicians may have never seen the front lines during World War II, the role they played in servicing the aircraft was as integral to the war effort as the pilots who flew the planes. There is a strong sense of duty and connection that mechanics and other service personnel feel toward the aircraft they work on—which may explain why one mechanic may not be willing to leave the base even though his tour of duty, the war, and his life have already passed.

During World War II, Cosford employed roughly 4,000 people. The famous Spitfire airplanes were assembled here, and in 1940 a large military hospital was constructed to assist with the repatriation of British prisoners of war. Today Cosford is also home to a military museum—its large hangars store some preserved war planes from the Second World War.

One of the highlights of the Cosford museum is the Lincoln Bomber, an imposing black bomber that was born too late to participate in World War II. Lincoln Bombers were conceived as more of a long-range bomber—an aircraft that could be used in the Pacific to reach Japan and then return safely to a non-hostile airfield. By the time the Lincolns were steadily rolling off of the assembly line, the war had ended. Lincolns were then considered for potential use in the Cold War, patrolling the edge of the Iron Curtain should a show of force become necessary. But as the Cold War escalated, so did the technology behind the weapons. The jet age had arrived in the 1950s, and the Lincolns were too slow and cumbersome to stand up to a jet fighter, and so they were phased out.

*The Lincoln Bomber.*
*Photo by Stuart Edmunds*

Lincoln Bomber No. RF398 arrived in Hangar 3 of the Cosford Museum in 1977 and is said to be haunted by a ghost. Some say the ghost is that of an airman in full flight suit who may have been the plane's pilot at one point in time. Others claim the ghost is a former engineer who seems bound to keep tinkering with the mechanics. Witnesses have reported seeing apparitions, and others said they heard the whistling of a tune, though no living source could be found. Though we can't be sure of who is haunting the hangar, we do know that the ghost accounts began shortly after the Lincoln arrived. Stuart Edmunds, a local paranormal investigator from Shropshire and also a former employee of the museum at Cosford, discussed some of the legends as well as his findings on the base.

"I'd never really heard of actual vehicles of any kind being haunted, and I was wondering how a plane would become haunted if it's not in one fixed position," Edmunds said. "Houses, because they've stood in the same place and the atmosphere and energies of past lives sort of congregate at that one space could explain why a house gets haunted. But how could a plane be haunted?"

That question was the beginning of his investigation here. Edmunds worked at the museum from January to August 2005 as a museum assistant. Though he couldn't get permission to do a full-on investigation of the planes and the hangar, he was granted permission to dig a little deeper into the ghosts here. "I used my position to try and get in there to do an investigation where I could spend the night around the Lincoln," he said. "It's quite surprising the number of noises that came out of the plane. It did sound like there were people in there playing with the dials even when the plane was completely locked up."

Edmunds was allowed inside the Lincoln to take a few pictures and to set up his recording equipment, which would be locked up for the night. The equipment would record until it ran out of tape.

*The Lincoln Bomber. Photo by Stuart Edmunds*

"What did you hear when you played the recordings back?" I asked.

"It sounded like buttons being pressed and almost like the crackle of a radio, that sort of thing," Edmunds said.

"Have any of the staff reported anything strange here?"

"I had a security guard tell me about an old lady in the hangar who said that she saw somebody in a World War II RAF uniform—like an engineer's uniform—with tools doing work on the Lincoln. She'd gone to security thinking that it was somebody that shouldn't be doing that work at that time of the day. The security guard went over and heard the sound of tools drop onto the floor, some footsteps across the hangar, and then a big massive bang against one of the fire doors—but he didn't see anything. They looked around, but there was no sign of any tools or anything, although there were some oil marks on the floor as if somebody had been working there. He said he couldn't explain it at all. He just assumed that there had been somebody probably obsessed with planes either trying to steal plane parts or just wanted to do it because he was an old engineer or something. This old lady was convinced that he had been dressed up in old clothes and it looked like he stepped straight out of 1945."

The Lincoln Bomber isn't the only haunted vehicle we've explored in *Ghosts of War*. What exactly is haunting these weapons of war isn't clear, and we can only speculate as to *why* planes and boats may be haunted. Perhaps the sense of duty from those who cared for vehicles such as the Lincoln Bomber ties them to these war relics, a sense of keeping the birds ready to fly at a moment's notice should England have the need.

# 27

# WORLD WAR II ARTIFACTS AND PARANORMAL ARCHAEOLOGY

**War:** World War II (1939–1945)

The ghosts of war haunt battlefields, buildings, and even boats and airplanes, but can they haunt the objects that these soldiers once held dear? Medals? Uniforms? A piece of a destroyed Sherman tank? Before we get too far, we need to cover two paranormal subjects at a high level: psychometry and dowsing.

Psychometry is the ability of some psychic or supernaturally sensitive persons to pick up on the people who owned or used an object. For example, if you own a ring and wear it every day for many years of your life, the theory is that some of your energy vibrations will be infused into the ring itself. Your personality, maybe even some profound scenes from your life, may be absorbed by this object that was dear to you. A psychic may hold your ring one day and get a sense of what you looked like, where you lived, possibly even tastes and smells that were significant in your life.

Dowsing, also known as divining or even witching, is a concept that is millennia old and is even referenced in the Bible—it's the ability to find something (I know "something" is not a very descriptive word, but stay with me for a minute) using some kind of pointer tool. When most people think of dowsing, they think of people who look for underground water sources using a forked tree branch or maybe L-shaped metal rods. By focusing their intent on finding underground water, a dowser moves around an area of land and the forked stick or L-shaped rods react when the dowser is standing over a vein of water. Dowsers don't just look for water; they have been known to look for underground oil, treasures, precious gems, lost items, and even subtle supernatural energies. In addition to forked sticks and L-shaped rods, dowsers may also use a pendulum, which is simply a weighted object at the end of a string or chain. The pendulum reacts when it's over whatever the dowser is looking for.

Richard Kimmel is a paranormal researcher who has been studying the psychometry of World War II artifacts since 2004. The 71-year-old lives in East Brunswick, New Jersey, and has been interested in objects from the Great War since 1945 when the then-10-year-old was given a German badge from his barber who had just returned from the war. When World War II ended, many United States GIs brought back souvenirs from the battlefront—medals taken from their fallen enemy, bullet shells, machine parts, pieces of uniforms, and anything else that would fit in their duffel bags. Over the years, a market for some of these items developed, and Kimmel found himself at various war paraphernalia trade shows combing through items for his collection. "I collected artifacts over the years and never thought much about them, except that when I held some of them I got a strange feeling from them," Kimmel said. "This was going on for years, but I never thought anything of it because I knew nothing of the paranormal. So I didn't know whether there was a connection or not."

After Kimmel underwent cardiac surgery in July 2004, his perspective on life changed a bit. He was watching a television program where people were using pendulums. He noticed the objects swung in counterclockwise directions, but only for some of the people on the program who tried it. "I was thinking about this, and two days later in the mail I received a tiny blessed wooden cross from a religious organization," Kimmel said. "They sent it to me for a contribution I had sent them. I said to myself, 'Just for the heck of it, I'll make a pendulum out of the cross.' So what I did was I made a hole in the top of it and I attached a piece of cotton string to it.

"I took a photograph that was taken at my daughter's wedding of my son-in-law, my daughter, and my dad, who since that time had passed on.

It was a large photograph—8x10—and the heads were fairly large. I held the pendulum over my daughter's head and there was no rotation. I held it over my son-in-law's head and there was no rotation. When I held it over my dad's head, it began to rotate in a clockwise direction."

Kimmel wanted to test his pendulum dowsing further, so he took out his high school yearbook. His 50th reunion was coming up, so his classmates were on his mind. He held the pendulum over the photographs and noticed that over some pictures nothing happened, and over others, it swung in a clockwise direction. He made notes of which pictures sent the pendulum spinning. When he got to the reunion, he looked at the bulletin board that displayed enlarged yearbook photos of those who had died from his graduating class. "It matched my list exactly," he said. "To me it was giving me a death indication somehow. So I started using it over several artifacts I had. I said, 'Let me see what happens.'"

*Richard Kimmel holds his blessed cross pendulum over the Sherman tank track coupling. Photo courtesy of Richard Kimmel*

During this same time period, Kimmel's daughter had formed a paranormal research group in New Jersey, so he was learning about psychic and supernatural phenomena while experimenting with pendulum dowsing. "I decided to take one of these artifacts and let their group take a look at it," Kimmel said. "I knew certain things about the artifact. I knew basically where it had come from. This particular one was a tank track coupling from a Sherman tank that was blown to pieces in the Northern Ardennes at the beginning of the Battle of the Bulge right on the famed Siegfried Line—in that area. I had a very strong rotation over this piece, so I knew there was a lot of energy connected to it. A psychic in my daughter's group examined it and she told me many things that I knew. She had no pre-knowledge of what this piece of metal was, but she told me that there were men running around yelling. Some had a grayish-type uniform, others had green uniforms—she was describing to me German forces and U.S. forces. At the time she had no way of knowing what this piece was or where it had come from. And she said she saw columns of vehicles and there were several people that were trying to communicate with her, or seemed to be trying to indicate something—I think it was more residual than anything. There were individuals, there were four or five of them, that seemed to be connected to this piece. I'm putting two and two together and thinking it could be the tank crew, because this tank was blown to pieces and there with chunks of armor plating that were found only the size of your fist. It was just strange what she was telling me about it. She said the column of trucks seemed to be moving very fast. From what I gather, I'm presuming from where I knew it came from, and from what she was telling me about it, that the trucks were part of the 106th infantry division. And they were moving rather rapidly because they were retreating. This got me going with other pieces."

*Hand-carved walnut symbol necklace.*
*Photo by Richard Kimmel*

The artifacts in Richard Kimmel's collection include identification bracelets, pieces of uniforms, old photographs of soldiers and officers, medals, badges, and many other pieces of military history. During our conversation, we focused on two of the pieces that are in the early stages of his investigation.

The infamous swastika that adorned Nazi Germany's flags has come to be known as a symbol of evil. It's important to note that neither Hitler nor the Germans invented this symbol, and its origins are significantly more pious. The traditional swastika is considered a holy symbol in Hinduism, Jainism, and Buddhism and is usually displayed either right-facing or left-facing with all lines positioned either straight up-and-down, or left-and-right. In the Nazi version, the symbol is twisted 45 degrees. This hand-carved walnut swastika has a loop at the top of one of its sides so it would be displayed in the traditional Hindu fashion. However because the entire symbol is hand-carved, it would have been difficult to carve the loop at the tip of one of the points. Kimmel believes this necklace to be Nazi in origin considering where it came from.

"This piece was taken from a German POW on D-Day at Ste Mere-Eglise, France, by a Sergeant of the 3rd Battalion, 505th Infantry, 82nd Airborne Division on June 6, 1944," Kimmel said. "The gentleman I got this from said all he really knew about it was that his uncle gave it to him before his death and told him that he got it in Ste Mere-Eglise, France, on D-Day. That's all he knew."

The town of Ste Mere-Eglise stood between Cherbourg and Caen and was occupied by the German army during World War II. The United States 82nd Airborne planned to drop in by parachute under the cover of darkness and take the village, cutting off German communication and blocking the main route between Cherbourg and the bulk of the German forces. But something went horribly wrong for the 82nd Airborne. First, the men were dropped too close to the town and were falling directly on top of it. The German sentries heard the airplane engines above and noticed the falling chutes almost immediately. The Germans fired at the slowly-sinking 82nd Airborne men, and many died before ever touching the ground. During night combat, it was common for machine guns to hold tracer bullets—ammunition that looks just like a regular bullet but carries a chemical compound (usually white phosphorus) that glows whitehot once the bullet is fired. The streaks of light look almost like lasers and help machine gunners find their targets in the darkness. Some of the tracers fired by the Germans that evening in Ste Mere-Eglise started a fire in a local farmhouse, and some unfortunate United States soldiers fell into the fire where they were burned to death. Others whose parachutes were caught in trees or on buildings were shot and killed, and those who made it to the ground were captured by the Germans.

After the short battle had ended, the Germans went back to sleep for the evening—a critical mistake, considering some 180 U.S. paratroopers had made it safely to the ground outside of town. The commander of the 3rd Battalion, 505th, Lt. Col. Ed Krause, quickly gathered the stray U.S. soldiers and slipped into town unnoticed. A local Frenchman showed Krause the German quarters, and the United States forces stormed in capturing 30 Germans, killing 10 others, and sending the rest fleeing into the woods. By dawn, the town was under United States control.

Kimmel isn't sure if the gold chain is original to the piece or not, but he does know that when he held his pendulum over the swastika, he saw a strong reaction. His paranormal investigation into this piece is just beginning, so he has no conclusions yet, but part of his testing procedure will include photographing the item from many angles. He will also employ a technique called "reflective photography" whereby he takes a photograph of the item through a mirror—the idea being that sometimes a paranormal anomaly may show up in the mirror that may give some insight into the item itself. He will also leave an audio recording device near the item in the still of the night to see if he can capture any Electronic Voice Phenomena (EVP) that may be attached to the item. And finally he will bring the swastika to a psychic in order to get her psychometric impressions of the item.

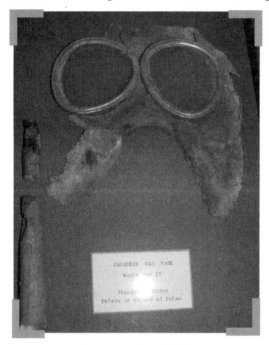

*Japanese Gas Mask.*
*Photo by Richard Kimmel*

One of the most intriguing pieces in Kimmel's collection is a World War II Japanese gas mask that was found in a cave on the Palau Island of Peleliu in the South Pacific. He came into possession of the item in the spring of 2005. "I received a phone call from an individual who was told about me by his cousin who attended one of the military shows that I was at," he said. "This fellow was getting some pretty bad vibes from the gas mask. He claims that he was hearing what he called mysterious voices. And what made it more interesting to me is that this was located by accident by the grandfather of the individual who I purchased it from. He didn't want much for it, he said, 'Send me $10 and it's yours. I just want to get rid of it.' He claims he heard voices at night from the room where the gas mask was in. The voice was saying something to the effect of 'I'm looking for help'—almost like the spirit that's connected to the piece wants to go home. And the fellow that had it is also psychic, he's both clairvoyant and clairaudient, but he has not seen the individual for some reason. But he said what he heard sounded like sort of a 'help me' type of message."

"Was the voice in English?" I asked.

"He said it was in a very broken type of English, like an Asian would speak broken English. That's what he said it sounded like."

The gas mask was found by the grandfather of the gentleman who sold Kimmel the item. This man had fought in the South Pacific campaign known as Bloody Nose Ridge, and he returned to the island in the 1990s to see where he once fought. He walked into one of the many caves along the waterfront and found the piece of the mask and shell casing pictured on page 202.

The Bloody Nose Ridge campaign involved intense fighting in the Palau Islands. On the island of Peleliu specifically, there was a garrison of 13,500 Japanese troops stationed there. A vast network of tunnels connected Japanese defenses, and over 500 caves on the island were fortified for defense. These islands were of strategic importance to the United States and its allies because they were considered a crossroad in the western Pacific. By knocking the Japanese out of the Palau Islands, allied forces could cut off and isolate the Japanese force on New Guinea and drive the Japanese back north into the Philippines and ultimately back to their own country. The Emperor of Japan knew this, and ordered the islands defended at all costs. In September of 1944, 800 American ships carrying 202,000 seamen and 1,600 aircraft circled the islands 10 miles out. The attack was scheduled for 8 AM on September 15.

Through the intense heat and crossfire, U.S. marines battled the dugin Japanese. For over a month, the operation continued with American forces searching the caves and tunnels until the Japanese were wiped out, which turned out to be a costly endeavor. The United States suffered 9,800 casualties and the Japanese over 13,000. Less than 300 Japanese were taken prisoner—many chose suicide over capture.

"When I received this piece, I immediately put the pendulum to it," Kimmel said. "I'll tell you, I've never gotten such a strong reaction from a pendulum in my life yet so far. I think if it could've flown off of the string, it would've done so. Very, very high energy coming from this. Very strong. What I did next was to leave it in my office overnight.

"I started about midnight when everything was quiet and everyone was in bed. I closed the door after I put my tape recorder on voice-activate, which was a mistake to begin with, but it did catch something. The tape shut off very quickly. During the recording it had picked up a sound—a banging type of sound, but nothing in the house could've made that. No car could've made that because the room is far from the street and the house is very soundproof. So it couldn't have been any outside sounds coming in. There was no voice, nothing other than this loud bang. I decided what I was going to do from there was to photograph the piece."

After examining the photograph he took with his digital camera, Kimmel noticed something in the mask's right lens (the left lens if you were wearing the mask, the right lens if you are facing it). When he zoomed in, he saw what appeared to be a small face. "I enlarged the image and I lightened and enhanced it to see it, and it definitely looks like a face to me—it looks slightly of an Asian or Japanese soldier with the type of headgear that they wore with the cloths coming out, and I can see part of his upper torso."

The next steps in the investigation process for the Japanese gas mask will include running a black light over it to see if some of the dark markings are bloodstains or simply rust from years of lying against a rock or piece of metal; further photographs of the piece using regular and reflective photography techniques; filming the mask with the near-infrared setting on his daughter's video camera; and then turning the piece over to a psychic for her impressions. "It's probably the most interesting piece that I have because of what I've been told about it and what I've seen so far myself. If I can get a name from whatever spirit is attached to this, I might be able to follow it up. Hopefully I can, but it can take quite a long time."

# Part XIII

Post-World War II

# (CIRCA 1947)

# 28

# THE PHANTOM SENTRY

**War:** Post-World War II
**Date of incident:** 1947
**Location:** Israel

War stories and strange tales of what has happened to soldiers on duty have been passed around for as long as there have been battles. If we hear one of these accounts from the source—or from someone who witnessed the events personally—we can give the story a lot more credibility. Folklore is a wonderful part of our lives, but as stories get further from the source, embellishments come in to play, and sometimes what actually happened is buried in the murky depths of storytelling.

I found the following account intriguing because it was passed from father to son and then told to me. Phil H., who asked that his surname not be used, describes his father as a very level-headed man—"boringly responsible" was how he put it. Phil was shocked when his father told him he'd once seen a ghost while stationed at a camp during his British Military service. The year was 1947 and British forces were occupying what would become the state of Israel. Phil's father and his fellow soldiers were guarding prisoners at this camp. Phil said:

"Dad was due on guard duty in a gun tower, complete with a search light and everything. There was one set of stairs to the tower and a little room at the top. So the duty guard would have to come down first. This duly happened, but in those few seconds Dad decided he needed to use the bathroom, so he asked the first guard to pop back up. He then went to the bathroom, returning to clearly see a soldier in the tower. The duty corporal then appeared and enquired as to why Dad was not in the tower. Dad replied that the previous guard had gone back for a moment, but the corporal put a spanner in the works by informing Dad that the previous duty guard was drinking tea in the Guardhouse. The duty NCO [Non Commissioned Officer] and my dad evidently both had the same thought: 'Who, then, is in the tower?' They shouted up, but received no reply. Both men ran up the stairs to the tower, but found it empty.

"It transpired that a passing sergeant had also seen the phantom sentry, and here's where the story takes an interesting twist: the sergeant had made a note to give the sentry a verbal thrashing as he clearly saw the man had a bayonet fixed to his rifle. This practice had been outlawed some weeks previous as another sentry had become bored and messed around with the searchlight, accidentally touching a wire with his bayonet. The man was killed instantly. Was the phantom sentry this man who showed up for one last guard duty? Dad doesn't know and, presumably, neither does the army, as nothing more was ever seen. Incidentally, Dad did not face an absence charge, as the duty corporal swore that there was a man in the tower."

# *Part XIV*

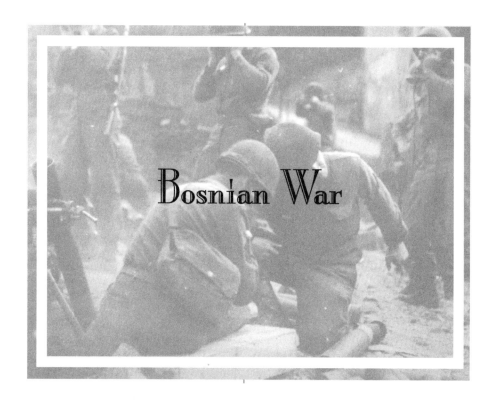

Bosnian War

*(1992–1995)*

# 29

# POSOVINA CORRIDOR

**War:** Bosnian War
**Dates of conflict:** April 1992–September 1995
**Location:** Bosnia and Herzegovina
**Participants:** Bosnians, Croats, and Serbs; United States, Russian, and other NATO forces also participated in post-war peacekeeping
**Casualties:** During the entire conflict, roughly 100,000 were killed, 40,000 raped, and 1.8 million people were displaced

> . . . *Retaining control of the Posovina corridor was and remains the key strategic objective of the Bosnian Serbs. The corridor serves as the link between the eastern and western halves of the Republika Srpska and maintaining full control of Brcko, which straddles the corridor, and its environs, is key to that objective . . . There appears to be some, but precious little maneuver room between the demands of both sides. Dissatisfaction on this key territorial issue could sow the seeds for future conflict in the area.*
> —Army Lieutenant General Patrick Hughes,
> August 1, 1996

There is a long history of the supernatural on the battlefield. Some soldiers have interpreted the experience to be angelic in origin, some kind of divine protection or message. But some encounters seem neither good nor evil—they just are.

The Bosnian War saw the most horrific bloodshed on European soil since World War II. Bosnia-Herzegovina is the name for the land that is formerly Yugoslavia. During the Cold War, Yugoslavia provided a land buffer between the Soviet Union and other European countries, so investment in Yugoslavia helped fuel a level of prosperity for the countries' people, which held the Muslim, Catholic, and Serbian people there at peace. After the Cold War, the outside money dried up almost overnight and the country crumbled. Yugoslavia was splitting up into separate countries, and where the borders would fall and who would live within them was a point of contention. Both the Bosnians and the Croats blame the Serbs for the start of the fighting that led to the war. Serbian president Slobodan Milosevic played up the ethnic differences and encouraged Serbs to band together against oppressing Muslims, who made up the majority of Bosnia, and Catholics, who made up the majority of Croatia. Milosevic wasn't the first and probably won't be the last leader to aim his citizens' discord against an ethnic group when the real problem is a lack of opportunity at home.

The Bosnian War led to many atrocities, ethnic cleansing, and mass rape. On November 21, 1995, a peace accord was drafted at Wright-Patterson Air Force base near Dayton, Ohio. Leaders from Bosnia, Serbia, and Croatia agreed to have 60,000 NATO peacekeeping troops move in. Twenty thousand of these forces would be Americans. One of those American servicemen was Calvary Scout Elmer Kilred (he is using a pseudonym to protect his identity), who was with the 1st Armored Division. Kilred and his comrades were the first group to cross into and secure the area of the Posovina Corridor—an area the Bosnian Muslims and Bosnian Serbs hotly contested.

"I was deployed in December of 1995," Kilred said. "I was a scout in a scout unit that was required to perform route reconnaissance for the movement of the First Armored Division into the former republics of Yugoslavia. During the time our troop spent in the Posovina Corridor, we experienced unexplainable happenings.

"Our troop was encamped in a cattle pasture outside of a town that had been ethnically cleansed. The place was out in the country, and to access the location you had to have some sort of tracked vehicle to navigate the dirt roads in the area. Most of the places in the Posovina Corridor were abandoned due to the fighting. Between January and February of 1996, I do not remember getting too much sleep, as we were on patrol most of the time or nailing down and negotiating the withdrawal and cleanup of weapons and landmines from an area occupied by one of the various factions declaring turf.

"If snow and ice were not on the ground, it was so muddy that traveling by foot was a real hassle. Near our encampment, one of the sections had to be called back due to activity in the area. The section was relaying information up to command of a possible soldier/sniper in their area. The snow on the ground was loose and tracks in the ground were present, proving that someone was running around scouting our encampment from the empty town. The section saw the soldier inside one of the houses and proceeded to subdue him. With a fresh cover of snow on the ground, there were only one set of boot prints into the house. With a section of three Bradley Fighting Vehicles on the outside of the house on the road, and soldiers following the trail of boot prints, there was nowhere for this soldier to go. When the dismounted soldiers arrived at the room in the house where the soldier was, he was nowhere to be found. His tracks ended at the window and there were no places to hide. This was one of the many things we would encounter in Bosnia . . . this was just one of the things that happened to get reported up higher, which was not commented on other than the section was told to carry on and continue on their patrol."

Wartime is confusing, and emotions and tension can run high. Admittedly, some people can get confused. But we also need to remember that a soldier's senses are elevated because he is on duty, and observations and decisions made on those observations can mean the difference between life and death. This event wasn't the only unexplained phenomenon that Kilred encountered in the Posovina Corridor.

"A few weeks later, I was on guard duty on the front gate of our encampment with another soldier from our tanker platoon," he said. "We had a fire barrel to keep us dry and the snow had melted, leaving mud everywhere. Our four-hour shift was around its halfway point at 3 AM when we watched a Bosnian soldier trod though the mud up to the gate of our encampment. We could hear him coming up to the gate, and there was enough light to make out the uniform of the soldier. While I was covered by the other soldier, I walked to the gate to get a closer look at this soldier. He got to the gate and looked like he had been working in the same clothes for at least a month. This person seemed real, but there was a dead glare in his eyes . . . I read it as soldier fatigue, or the 100-mile stare. It's like he looked through me while looking at me. When I met the Bosnian soldier at the front gate, he just seemed interested in having a cigarette. I gave him one of mine and lit it for him. I leaned over the concertina wire to light the cigarette in his mouth while he shielded the wind from putting out my lighter. He waved and turned to leave, and so I turned around to leave the gate and the other guard who was with me freaked. He said, 'Where the *blank* did he go?' I turned around and the soldier had disappeared, cigarette and all. Me and the other soldier on duty looked for the guy, but the ember of the lit cigarette could not be seen, and the guy's tracks ended about 3 to 4 feet from where he was standing. We decided not to report the activity to our guard commander."

For Kilred, seeing a ghost wasn't the most frightening thing he witnessed in Bosnia. "It was the things that people did or had done to one another that gave me chills," he said.

# AFTERWORD

Thank you to those who served, who are serving, and to those who won't let us forget the past.

# GLOSSARY

**aerodrome**  An airfield.

**bastion**  The projecting part of a fortress; a fortified area or position.

**blockhouse**  A military fortification constructed of concrete or other sturdy material, with loopholes (small openings) for defensive firing or for observation.

**breastwork**  A temporary fortification.

**casement**  A window sash that opens outward by means of hinges.

**constabulary**  An armed police force organized like a military unit but distinct from the regular army.

**docent**  A person who leads guided tours through a museum or art gallery.

**dowsing**  The ability to find something using some kind of pointer tool.

**dreadnought**  A fast battleship that is armed with large-caliber guns.

**disarticulate**  To become disjointed.

**effigy**  A crude figure representing a hated person.

**interposition**  Intervention or intrusion; having put oneself between.

**invocation**  Incantation; the act or process of petitioning for help or support.

**paranormal**  Not within the range of normal experience or scientifically explainable phenomena; supernatural.

**psychometry**  Divination of facts concerning an object or its owner through contact with or proximity to the object.

**repatriation**  The restoration or return of a person to that person's country of origin, allegiance, or citizenship.

**sensitive** A person with psychic powers, without the ability to establish communication with the departed (in other words, not a medium); a person who is aware of and can detect paranormal events and can feel the presence of a spirit.

**sortie** A mission or attack by a single plane; raid or expedition.

**tracer bullet** Ammunition that looks like a regular bullet but carries a chemical compound (such as white phosphorus) that glows white-hot once the bullet is fired.

**veridical** Truthful or genuine.

**vilify** To utter slanderous and abusive statements against; defame.

# FOR MORE INFORMATION

The Alamo
P.O. Box 2599
San Antonio, TX 78299
(210) 225-1391
Web site: http://www.thealamo.org/main.html
The Web site provides information about the original Misión San
Antonio de Valero, the role of the Alamo during the Texas
Revolution, and details about the historic 1836 siege.

Antietam National Battlefield
National Park Service
P.O. Box 158
Sharpsburg, MD 21782
(301) 432-5124
Web site: http://www.nps.gov/anti
Information about the Battle of Antietam and schedules for
touring the battlefield are available on the National Park
Service's Web site.

Bran Castle Museum
Traian Mosoiu str., no. 489
Bran 507025
Romania
+40 268 238 333

Web site: http://www.brancastlemuseum.ro/indexfrm_en.htm
The official site for the Bran fortress, museum, and historical
archive, which provides information about the real Wallachia
ruler Vlad the Impaler and the fictional character Dracula, who
was created by Bram Stoker.


Fort Meigs
P.O. Box 3
29100 West River Road
Perrysburg, OH 43552
(800) 283-8916 or (419) 874-4121
Web site: http://www.fortmeigs.org
Fort Meigs is a War of 1812 battlefield that is operated today by the
Ohio Historical Society. The Web site provides information about
the fort's history and special events.


Gettysburg National Military Park
1195 Baltimore Pike, Suite 100
Gettysburg, PA 17325-2804
(717) 334-1124, ext. 8023
Web site: http://www.nps.gov/gett
The Civil War battlefield is maintained by the National Park Service.
The Web site includes information about the Civil War, the Battle
of Gettysburg (1863), and photographs from the battle and other
Civil War artifacts.


USS *Arizona* Memorial
1 Arizona Memorial Place
Honolulu, HI 96818
(808) 422-0561
Web site: http://www.nps.gov/usar
The National Park Service provides information about the battleship
that was sunk on December 7, 1941, and honors the place where
World War II started for the United States.

# Web Sites

Due to the changing nature of Internet links, Rosen Publishing has developed an online list of Web sites related to the subject of this book. This site is updated regularly. Please use this link to access the list:

http://www.rosenlinks.com/hgp/gow

# FOR FURTHER READING

Austin, Joanne. *Weird Hauntings: True Tales of Ghostly Places* (Weird). New York, NY: Sterling, 2006.

Bakewell, Lori. *Gettysburg Adventure: Ghost on the Battlefield*. Frederick, MD: PublishAmerica, 2005.

Belanger, Jeff. *Our Haunted Lives: True Life Ghost Encounters*. Franklin Lakes, NJ: New Page Books, 2006.

Glass, Debra Johnston, and Heath Mathews. *Skeletons of the Civil War: True Ghost Stories of the Army of Tennessee*. Florence, AL: Debra Glass, 2007.

Konstam, Angus. *Civil War Ghost Stories*. Chicago, IL: Thunder Bay Press, 2005.

Kwon, Heonik. *Ghosts of War in Vietnam* (Studies in the Social and Cultural History of Modern Warfare). New York, NY: Cambridge University Press, 2008.

Munn, Debra D. *Montana Ghost Stories*. Helena, MT: Riverbend Publishing, 2007.

Nesbitt, Mark. *Ghosts of Gettysburg: Spirits, Apparitions, and Haunted Places of the Battlefield*. Volume VI. Nashville, TN: Second Chance Publishing, 2004.

Oester, Dave, and Sharon Oester. *Ghosts of Gettysburg: Walking on Hallowed Ground*. Bloomington, IN: iUniverse, Inc., 2007.

Okonowicz, Ed. *Civil War GHOSTS at Fort Delaware*. Elkton, MD: Myst and Lace Publishers, Inc., 2006.

Rule, Leslie. *Ghosts Among Us: True Stories of Spirit Encounters*. Riverside, NJ: Andrews McMeel Publishing, 2004.

Rule, Leslie. *When the Ghost Screams: True Stories of Victims Who Haunt*. Riverside, NJ: Andrews McMeel Publishing, 2006.

# BIBLIOGRAPHY

Asfar, Dan. *Haunted Battlefields*. Edmonton, Alberta, Canada: Ghost House Books, 2004.

Bailey, Ronald H. *The Bloodiest Day: The Battle of Antietam*. Alexandria, VA: Time-Life Books, 1984.

Belanger, Jeff. *Communicating with the Dead: Reach Beyond the Grave*. Franklin Lakes, NJ: New Page Books, 2005.

Belanger, Jeff, ed. *Encyclopedia of Haunted Places: Ghostly Locales from Around the World*. Franklin Lakes, NJ: New Page Books, 2005.

Belanger, Jeff. *The World's Most Haunted Places: From the Secret Files of Ghostvillage.com*. Franklin Lakes, NJ: New Page Books, 2004.

Boyd, Thomas. *Mad Anthony Wayne*. New York, NY: Charles Scribner's Sons, 1929.

Cohen, Daniel. *Civil War Ghosts*. New York, NY: Scholastic, Inc., 1999.

Coleman, Christopher K. *Dixie Spirits: True Tales of the Strange and Supernatural in the South*. Nashville, TN: Cumberland House, 2002.

Fraser, Antonia. *The Gunpowder Plot: Terror and Faith in 1605*. London, England: Phoenix, 2002.

Grant, Ulysses S. *The Civil War Memoirs of Ulysses S. Grant*. Forge, New York, NY: A Tom Doherty Associates Book, 2002.

Hearn, Lafcadio. *Kwaidan: Stories and Studies of Strange Things*. New York, NY: Dover Publications, Inc., 1968.

Hitsman, J. Mackay. *The Incredible War of 1812: A Military History*. Toronto, Canada: Robin Brass Studio, 1999.

Kennedy, Frances H., ed. *The Civil War Battlefield Guide, Second Edition*. Boston, MA: Houghton Mifflin Company, 1998.

*Liverpool Echo.* "Blown away ... when I contacted Guy Fawkes Guy Fawkes; Janet Tansley speaks to TV psychic Derek Acorah about why his new show went with a real bang." By Janet Tansley, November 3, 2005.

Machen, Arthur. *The Bowmen and Other Legends of the War.* London, England: Simpkin, Marshall, Hamilton, Kent & Co., Ltd., 1915.

McPherson, James. M. *Crossroads of Freedom: Antietam: The Battle That Changed the Course of the Civil War.* Oxford, England: Oxford University Press, 2002.

*The Tennessean.* "Face in the window evokes McGavock child." By Peggy Shaw, July 1, 2002. Page 1W.

# INDEX

# ABOUT THE AUTHOR

Jeff Belanger leads a very haunted life. He's been fascinated with history and the supernatural since age 10, when he investigated his first haunted house during a sleepover. Since then, he's been a writer and journalist for various newspapers and magazines, and in 1999 he launched Ghostvillage.com as a repository for his writings on the subject of the supernatural. The Web site has since grown to become the largest paranormal resource on the Web, attracting hundreds of thousands of visitors per year.

Through Jeff's work as a journalist and a writer, he's had the opportunity to speak with hundreds of people from all over the world regarding the profound events that have changed their lives. His objective and open-minded approach to the subject makes the supernatural accessible to a wide audience. Jeff is a regular guest on many regional and national radio programs, lectures regularly across the United States, and has been featured on television programs about the paranormal. He currently haunts Massachusetts with his wife, Megan.